SHELLEY

SHELLEY

Peter Tilbury and
Colin Bostock-Smith

Based on the Thames television series
by Peter Tilbury

NEW ENGLISH LIBRARY/TIMES MIRROR

A New English Library Original Publication, 1980

First NEL Paperback Edition March 1980

NEL Books are published by
New English Library Limited from
Barnard's Inn, Holborn,
London EC1N 2JR.
Made and printed in Great Britain by
Hunt Barnard Printing Ltd.,
Aylesbury, Bucks.

45004931 0

ONE

THE FIRST thing I noticed about the waitress was her bosom. Come to think of it, that was all I noticed about her.

But it was a nice bosom. Big and comfy. Plump and pillowy. I was free to stare at it, too, partly because the lady herself was concentrating on writing out my bill – an activity, incidentally, which made those beautiful boobs bounce ever so slightly – and partly because Fran, who would normally nail me with her beady eye when I made similar surveys, was up to her lovely lashes in newsprint. That was the purpose of our presence in the café – to shelter from the elements while we searched the accommodation columns for . . . well, for accommodation. At least, Fran did the searching, because she is the active one of our partnership. She's the doer, the one with the get-up-and-go. Me, I'm the lazy bugger. We make a good team.

The waitress, who would have made a good team with Big Daddy, finished writing our bill with a final jerk of her pencil. Quiver, quiver!

'Tea and coffee?' she checked.

Fran said 'Yes' without looking up.

I said, 'I'm afraid we failed.'

'What?' said the waitress – and she gave me a look.

Now, I know that look. People give it to me all the time. It's a look that says: 'Hello! Something odd is happening! This feller with the fringe is a weirdo! Better watch out!' It's a look that I just can't resist.

'We drank them both slowly and carefully,' I told her, 'but we couldn't guess which was which.'

'Trying to be funny?'

I suppose 'Yes' was an honest answer, but in fact I said, 'One *was* a darker grey than the other.'

'What?'

'Tell me one thing – how do you manage to serve them both at blood heat?'

'Look . . .'

Room for one more. 'Do you stick your elbow in it?'

That was far enough for now, I decided. The bosom was beginning to heave with indignation.

'Look, it's not my fault, I only . . .'

'I know, I know.' I held up hands in surrender.

'All I do is serve the stuff. If you . . .'

'I'm sorry.' I gave her a sincere look in the eyes. 'It's early, I'm bad tempered.' A small smile. 'Forgive me.' A gentle hand on her arm, and the clincher: 'You do look lovely in that overall.'

'Oh, er . . .'

'Is that real Terylene?'

'Oh, yeah. Throughout.' She was really pleased.

'You look a picture.'

'Oh, thank you.'

Now leave it there, Shelley, I told myself. Enough is enough. Everyone's happy. She's a nice lady with a nice bosom, so be a nice chap and don't say any more. All right? Good.

Oh . . . but I can't resist. Never could.

So I put my other hand on Fran's, as it held *The Evening Standard*, and said to both girls at once, 'You don't fancy a bit of troilism, do you?'

If I'd hoped for a dual explosion of indignation, I was disappointed.

Fran said, 'Mmm?'

And the waitress said, 'We don't do meals till later. It's Moussaka à la grecque today.'

'Ah.'

'Or,' she added, 'Toad-in-the-hole.'

I tried not to laugh. 'That's nearer what I had in mind, actually.'

'I could do you a sandwich.'

That was even nearer what I had in my squalid little mind, but I declined with grace.

'No, thanks. The coffee was enough.'

She looked down her bosom at me. 'Yours was the tea, pay at the desk.' And she went, displaying a behind that was a considerable disappointment after the promise of the front.

'Thank you,' I muttered in her direction, and turned back to Fran, who was now showing signs of surfacing amongst her newspapers.

'What a good-natured, warm, intelligent chest that girl has got – did you notice?' I asked.

'There's only three . . . ' Fran said.

Three? Most girls are happy with two.

' . . . in here.' She meant *The Evening Standard.* 'I'll do those. Will you do that agency?'

I picked up one of the papers. The newsprint came off on my fingers, and the brightness went out of the morning. I hate looking for somewhere to live. It's depressing. Think of poor old Moses, wandering in the wilderness for umpteen years with the people of Israel until they found somewhere to live. No wonder he was such a moody old buzzard.

'Is there anything in those?' Fran asked, nodding at the paper I held.

I didn't have a clue. 'No,' I said. Then I showed her a picture of bloody Buzby in a GPO advertisement. 'Look at that! When did you last see an overweight canary phoning up his friends?'

'What?' said Fran.

People say 'what?' to me a lot. Even Fran.

'What is it about advertisers?' I asked her. 'Sex and twaddle is all they can think of. If it isn't the sun-drenched bit of cheesecake gazing at you in open-mouthed ecstasy over a bottle of Navy rum, it's a band of tweeting pixies checking your oil. I suppose sooner or later we'll have the ultimate advert – Busby making love to Raquel Welch. That should make the Post Office a multinational, and put Mary Whitehouse into . . .'

I went on for quite a bit like this. I often do. In some strange Zen-type way it helps.

'Bloody hell, Shelley,' said Fran in her practical way when I paused for breath, 'what are you going on about now?'

'Advertisers. They treat us all like a bunch of sex-obsessed infants. Look at this girl – traipsing about in a hopelessly inadequate bikini to plug do-it-yourself gear. I mean, I know some people are turned on by some pretty odd things, but what she's got to do with ready-cut plasterboard is beyond me . . .'

I was all set to be off again on this rather good-looking hobby-horse, when stone me if I didn't recognise the girl in the advertisement.

'Dear God in heaven, it's Sandra Ferguson!'

'It isn't!'

'Looks like her.'

'So it is.' Fran remembered Sandra. She had good reason to. Mind you, I had better reason.

'What on earth you were doing with her, Shelley, I'll never know,' Fran now remarked.

'Oh, I was a simple God-fearing male chauvinist pig in those days,' I recalled, 'and she made the hormones dance. I mean, she was perfectly pretty with flawless make-up, seven kinds of perfume . . .'

'And Polyfilla behind the eyes,' Fran put in with cruel accuracy. 'And,' she went on, 'fascinating though I find this in-depth discussion of your ex-affairs, I think it's time we looked for somewhere to live. I really would like to get on with some work.'

By 'work' Fran means writing. She's a novelist. So far she has written one-third novels. But one day she'll write a real cracker – we both know that – and then she'll be famous and rich and so on. It's bound to happen in time. Meanwhile . . .

'How's it going?' I asked.

'Terrible. I mean, even Jane Austen would find it difficult to write a novel in a two-roomed flat with four people.'

'Yeah. Pity Michael came back.'

'It is his flat, Shelley.' Ever notice how some people can't resist stating the obvious? 'He's been very good. We can't sleep on his floor much longer.'

'Well . . . ' God, I hate looking for somewhere to live.

'Shelley, we can't!' She wasn't arguing, she was telling me. 'We can't! It's so embarrassing.'

I grinned. 'No it isn't. We always wait until he's asleep.'

Fran ignored that, and perhaps it's just as well, because if pushed I'd have to admit that I only wait until Michael *appears* to be asleep, and it's easy enough to fake a snore. However . . .

Fran said doubtfully, 'I suppose we could stay at your mother's.'

I recoiled from the thought. 'I can't stand her pooffey boyfriend.'

'They're not there.'

'Poncey little house painter.' I really can't stand him.

'House *restorer*,' Fran corrected. 'They're skiing in Scotland.'

'Typical. I suppose he goes on safari in Windsor Great Park and scuba-diving in Whitestone Ponds.'

Fran gave me a look that said 'Shut up!' Aloud she said, 'Well, we could stay there for two weeks.'

'No point.' Gallantly, I faced reality. 'We've got to find somewhere sometime.'

A yawn crept up from nowhere and started to tie my arms in a knot behind my neck. 'These early mornings are killing me,' I told her.

'It's ten-thirty.'

'Oh God!' I remembered. 'I've got to collect my giro.'

'Why don't they post that?'

'Had to give a false address.'

We headed for open spaces, pausing for a second to pay the cashier.

'You'd have to go a long way for coffee like that,' I told him.

'Thank you, sir.' He was an innocent young Bengali, but why should I be merciful?

'Like a motorway service station,' I finished. And left.

Next stop – the Labour Exchange. But before I get there, there's something I ought to say.

If you are one of those people who think that our Welfare State is a disgrace, that people who sponge off the State are criminal, that wasters and layabouts who receive free handouts ought to be horsewhipped around the county and have their nasty bits chopped off and hung on Tower Bridge . . .

. . . if you are one of those people, then I first congratulate you on your perspicacity, and then advise you to give up on me now. Because I am one of them spongers.

That's where my giro comes in. Those of you who earn an honest crust may not know that this is how the money comes to most of us spongers – by giro cheque through the post. Only mine doesn't, because I gave a false address. Why did I give a false address? I'll tell you later.

The point is, I pick up my cheque, in person, from the fair-ish hand of a Mr Alan Forsyth, employee of the local Labour Exchange. Which is what I should have been doing at nine of the clock that morning.

But instead it was nearly eleven when I found myself face to face with Forsyth. I was late – an almost unforgivable crime in the world of the Department of Employment. Now this Forsyth chap would be a vindictive bastard if he was bright enough, and I can see his eyes gleaming as he checks his watch and waits for me to reach the counter. He wants to give battle. Isn't he a silly little man? Doesn't he know he's tangling with a professional?

'You should have signed at nine this morning, Mr Shelley.' Pretty weak for an opening salvo, I thought.

'Had to drive me mother to work.'

'Really?' Sneer, sneer. 'What sort of work does your mother do?'

'Foreman on a building site.'

'Mr Shelley . . .' Once they start 'Mr Shelley'-ing you, they're on the retreat.

'She has to be driven, you see,' I continued, 'on account of her wooden leg.'

He withdrew in reasonable order, swallowed, adjusted tie, eased crutch, and began again.

'I'm glad your sense of humour hasn't deserted you, Mr Shelley. How is it that an educated, intelligent young man like yourself manages to remain unemployed for so long?'

'It's just a knack. Anyone could do it.'

He picked up my file card and read through it, thus avoiding my eye.

'According to this you took a degree *and* a PhD, and since then you've never worked at all, except for a holiday job as a bean packer.'

Yes, it's true, I was a bean packer. Oh those tins!

'Working on my biography?' I asked Forsyth.

He mounted a serious attack. 'Do you know how many people are unemployed in this country?'

Did I know? Of course I knew. I've got one of those minds.

'After seasonal adjustment,' I told him, 'one million, three hundred and twelve thousand.'

I enjoyed the pause that followed.

'Quite,' said Forsyth with an effort. 'Many of them without your qualifications. Desperate for a job.'

I looked at him with amazed innocence. 'Would you like me to take a job away from one of them?'

Forsyth now went for simplicity. 'You're a nutcase, Mr Shelley!'

I drew myself up. 'You want to be less rude to your regulars, mate. It's us hard-core layabouts that's your bread-and-butter.'

'Mr Shelley . . .'

'I mean, we put up with a lot, you know – all these kids, straight from school, still wet behind their punk hairstyles and straight on the dole at the full rate, no differentials at all, very hard for us senior men to take.' I was in full swing now, and enjoying it. 'Once the government get the economy rolling again – and it won't be long now, the politicians were all most optimistic during the election – once that's happened all these weekend layabouts will be swept away, and they'll do a Beeching on all these places. Oh yes, there'll be a queue of trendies buying them up for middle-class housing. And you will be the only people unemployed. *Then* you'll be sorry . . . '

I paused for a moment while Forsyth swayed under the impact of it all, and then, ' . . . as you watch the pigs flying about in the trees. By the way, Mr . . . ?'

Automatically, he said, 'Forsyth.'

'Bruce?' It couldn't be. He hadn't fallen *that* low.

'Alan.'

'Alan Forsyth.' I gave the name a dignity its owner lacked, and thrust my hand across the counter. 'How d'you do. Now, as I've been signing here regularly now for . . .'

'Sixty-nine weeks,' Forsyth said faintly.

'As you say, sixty-nine weeks, I wondered if I qualified for holiday pay.'

Forsyth 'Mr Shelley'd' me again.

'Call me James. Nobody ever does.'

Another 'Mr Shelley'.

'In lieu, you see,' I said reasonably. 'Because I didn't get a chance to go away this year, and . . .'

Forsyth escaped sideways from all this by finding my giro envelope on the counter, and asking, 'Why don't we post this to you?'

'Where I live the mail gets stolen.'

Now he thinks he's caught me. 'According to this . . .' – my card – 'you live with your mother.'

'She's a kleptomaniac.'

Sometimes it's so easy, I'm ashamed of myself. Forsyth sighed. I think it was a sigh. It might have been a sob.

'Which is a drag,' I continued, ''cos with the wooden leg she's not too hot on the getaways.' I got my hands on the giro before that did a getaway, then went on. 'I say, you couldn't manage a bit more, could you? No? How about a productivity deal? I sign twice a week and fill in a few extra C-17s?'

'Goodbye, Mr Shelley.' Forsyth's eyes had gone glassy.

'Bye now. See you next week if I'm spared.'

Forsyth made one last attempt. 'If you could manage to sign on at the proper time next week it would help us. I mean, I know it's a strain for you, week in and week out, but if it's no trouble . . . sorry to have to ask.' The sarcasm dripped down and formed a pool on the counter.

I gave him a quizzical look. 'You sure you're not Bruce Forsyth?'

TWO

COMING UP – Nasty Experience of the Day, Number One. It happened at the accommodation agency.

I suppose there have to be such things as accommodation agencies. They must exist. Life's rich pattern has to encompass really nasty places, such as British Rail buffets, or tramps' armpits, or . . . accommodation agencies.

But if I had a choice between those last two, I'd take the tramps' armpits.

There was a black guy before me in the queue at the agency, and his opinion of the place must make mine seem mild in comparison. The agent himself, a wormy little man with yellow fingers, dealt with him in the following manner:

'Yes sir, what can I do for you?'

'I'd like a small flat for me and my wife.'

'Sorry, sir, nothing in at the moment.'

'Nothing at all?'

'Sorry, sir.'

'But . . .'

'Awfully sorry. Look in again.'

'Yeah.'

And that was that. No small flats available. Out went the black guy. And I got to my feet, heading in the same direction. But Weasel-features called me back.

'Yes, sir? Can I help you?'

'Well, I gather not. I want the same as him.'

'Sit down, sir. Flat for you and your wife?'

'Girlfriend,' I corrected. 'Small flat. Big bed-sit.'

He nodded encouragingly, and began sorting through papers. 'Well, let's see what we can do . . .'

'But . . . ' I gestured wordlessly towards where the black guy had been.

A look of prim and secret satisfaction spread across the man's mottled cheeks. 'I have to match the tenant to the accommodation, sir. That's my job. Name?'

'James Shelley. Look . . .'

Of course I should have walked out. Racialism survives because we fail to kill it off. To accept it is to support it. Here was a chance to make a personal stand against a cruel prejudice. I *should* have walked out. But . . . Fran and I had to have somewhere to live. We were desperate. Maybe the creep behind the desk could find us somewhere. So I didn't walk out. James Shelley, internationalist, brother of all men, swallowed a principle and sat tight. Sometimes I really *am* ashamed of myself. My God, I hate looking for somewhere to live.

'What do you do for a living?' asked Face-ache.

Well, I wasn't going to dignify the man by lying to him. 'I'm unemployed.'

'Civil Servant . . . ' and he wrote the words on a card. 'References?'

'What?'

'Present landlord?'

'Well . . .'

'Say you live with your mother, that's safest.'

Good grief, who was this guy? Me? – I was ashamed I'd ever used that line about my mother.

'Personal reference?'

'Ah . . . ' Strange. When you decide to tell the truth, you sometimes can't think of anything to say. However, the insect opposite had no such problems.

'If there's any problem, give them our tenants' number, and say you've known Mr Hutchings for years. I'll sort it out.'

'Yes. I see. Mr Hutchings.' I began to itch with the unpleasantness of it all.

'For you and your girlfriend?'

'Yes.'

A slight prurient gleam in the weak eyes. 'You're not planning a family, are you?'

'No.'

'Jolly good. That's all right then.'

I felt uncomfortable, as if I'd been co-operating in something underhanded, deceitful and unpleasant. What am I on about? I *had* been co-operating in something underhanded, deceitful and unpleasant. And now the thing had got personal – this dreadful creep was pleased that I didn't plan on having children.

I dredged up some irony. 'Perhaps I'd best pop out and have the operation first. Just to be on the safe side.'

'Mmm?' He was crossing out names on a brightly coloured sheet of paper.

'Surprised you haven't got the facilities on the premises.'

It was wasted. He wasn't listening. Instead he handed me the sheet of paper covered with addresses, along with a simple form. Both felt tacky.

'Here you are – complete list. Sign here.' A slight guilty pause, then, 'If we find you somewhere we charge two weeks' rent.'

I looked at him. 'But that's against the law.'

He stared back. 'Mustn't let ourselves be hidebound by bureaucracy.'

His hand twitched, and he had retrieved his coloured paper. The form lay in front of me. Stalemate.

Oh, what the hell! In for a penny, in for two weeks' rent. I signed. Got up. Went.

And as I went I could hear Ferret-face babbling into the phone . . .

'Hello? Mr Hutchings speaking . . . Known him for years, most reliable, quiet, honest fellow. Can't speak too highly of . . .'

So let us now move away from the seedy business section of the metropolis, away to the green and pleasant residential windowboxes of West Hampstead, and to a meeting that was to be of lasting significance in the life of J. Shelley, of no fixed abode.

Have you ever met someone new, and known deep within you that from then on the lives of you and that someone will be intertwined, that you will come to know each other intimately, that for good or evil you have been flung together by the whirl of fate, etcetera, etcetera? You know the feeling? Well, there in West Hampstead that morning I met Mrs Hawkins, and you know, I don't think either of us felt a thing like that.

We both felt plenty of other emotions.

Mrs Hawkins met me at the front door of her charming home. I knew it was a charming home, because the door was fringed with net curtains, the bell-push chimed, and on the wall just inside there was a picture of some white horses thundering through surf. Mrs Hawkins herself was obviously one of telly-land's busy housewives – indeed, I could hear her washing machine thundering through Surf at that very moment – but she was as charming and gracious as her home, and only too happy to spare a little time for someone who might shortly be paying her a great deal of money every week.

She led the way upstairs to the 'flatlet', while I summed up my impressions of her. Fortyish face on a thirtyish body that spoke of too much nervous energy. The eyes were landlady's eyes – bright, piercing, not even trusting their own evidence – and her voice was that of the woman who sits behind you on the bus and tells her friend about her operation. Sort of . . . shrill. To be blunt, Mrs Hawkins was not the type to fulfil my fantasies of the 'older woman', but . . .

. . . but the room she had to let was not bad at all. It might be just what Fran and I needed.

Mrs H. led the way in, turned, folded her arms, and got down to business.

'Where did you say you were employed, Mr Shelley?'

As an opening gambit, I thought that a little unfair. But I fought back, as by now you would expect me to do.

'Lovely pullover.'

Instinctively she glanced down at herself, down at pointed breasts that were a tribute to the two-way stretch.

'Oh, thank you,' she stuttered.

'Is that genuine acrylic?'

'Oh yes, a hundred per . . . ' and then she caught herself. No pushover, this one. No bat-brained waitress. 'What?'

'I'm on the government payroll.'

'Oh really? What department?' I *think* she believed me.

'Department of Employment.'

'What, the one just down the road from here?'

'Yes.' It was, too. The place could not be more handy. Within such easy reach of the money supply.

Mrs H. agreed. 'Well,' she said, 'that would be convenient for you then. What's your position with them?'

The correct answer was 'tenuous', but instead I said, 'I'm involved in unemployment statistics.' Which was also correct.

She nodded approval. 'That's nice and steady then, isn't it.'

'Certainly got a future, anyway.'

Her brow furrowed suddenly with emotion. 'Makes me boil, all this unemployment!'

'It is dreadful,' I agreed. And wondered. What was this? Had I unearthed a radical landlady? A deep-red Trotskyist in blue acrylic and yellow rinse, fuming at the prospect of decent working people thrown out of work by capitalism?

I should co-co.

'Half of them layabouts. Gerrin' money for nuffin'. Makes you sick.'

Ah yes, of course. Familiar territory after all.

I began, 'Well . . . ' without a clue what else I could say, but Mrs H. had had enough of politics for the moment.

'Where are you living now?'

'Sorry?'

'In case I wanted a reference.'

I wasn't going to give her the name from the agency. Low I might be, but I clung to some tattered remains of self-respect. My only alternative, however, was to wheel out the aged parent again.

'I live with my mum.'

Mistake! She *was* a bit sharp, this one, and she was on it like a flash. 'Ah! Then why are you looking . . . '

I thought quickly. 'That is, I did. I mean, she died.' Mentally, I apologised to mother.

'Oh I am sorry, how dreadful for you,' said Mrs H., her voice heavy with insincerity.

'Well, a release in some ways. Her leg gave her a lot of trouble, you know.' It was giving me quite a bit, too.

'And you want the flat for yourself?'

'Yes.'

'Fine.' She smiled. Nice teeth.

'And my wife.'

'Ah . . . ' Teeth disappeared, to be replaced by two thin red lips. 'It's quite a small flat.'

I smiled. 'We're very close.'

'Yes, but . . . '

I put on my Bob Monkhouse voice – the warm velvet tones of total humbug. 'I mean, you know, we'd like to live together. If possible. I think it's nice, that – don't you?'

'Well, of course, but . . . '

'Are you married?'

'Well, yes, but . . . '

'Your husband lives here, does he?'

'Well, yes, but . . . '

'There you are, you see . . . ' By now my smile was more Liberace than Monkhouse, 'Case in point.'

'Mr Shelley . . . ' Like Mr Forsyth, she was on the retreat when she said that. Time to get over a rather difficult hurdle.

'Actually,' I said casually, 'she's not my wife.'

'Pardon?' Well, at least she didn't scream or faint.

'Fran.'

'Look, Mr Shelley . . . '

'Common law,' I admitted, 'but . . . '

'I'm not worried about that,' said Mrs H. So it wasn't such a difficult hurdle after all.

'It *is* a double bed,' I remarked, eyeing the item itself speculatively.

'Yes.' Non-committal.

'Pity to waste it.'

I think for a moment Mrs H. began to wonder just where this conversation was leading. It certainly wasn't going the way she intended. She squared her shoulders, and looked me straight in the eye.

'You see . . . ' she began. But I got in first.

'Is that moulding coming away?'

'What?' Like I said, people say 'what?' to me all the time.

I pointed up at the cornice. 'Can be expensive in these old houses, too.'

She tried again: 'Mr Shelley . . . '

'Call me James. No one ever does.'

'Mr Shelley . . . ' She was getting shriller.

'Oh, no.' I looked closer at the ceiling. 'No, all it needs is a spot of polythix high yield.'

I've always believed that the phrase 'polythix high yield' would stop a rhino at forty paces. It stopped Mrs H. all right. But then she's hardly in the rhino class. More your elk, really. However . . .

'What?' she said again.

'Polythixotropic high yield adhesian aggregate,' I explained. 'Wonderful stuff. I should get that done before it spreads.'

I'd got her going now. 'Get what done?' she asked, looking round in a flap.

'Don't let them charge you much, mind. Hardly anything needs doing at the moment.'

'You done decorating and that then?'

'Trained as a house restorer.' I nearly fluffed on 'restorer' but she didn't notice, especially as I was pointing at the ceiling, sucking my teeth, and going on to say, 'Oh no, that's not serious.'

Mrs H. made a couple more false starts, then finally got around to what she wanted to say in the first place.

'I did want to let it to a single.'

'Of course. Quite understand.'

'But I really don't see . . . '

'Thank you very much.' I put finality into my voice. 'It's a nice flat.' I started to back away.

'Well, look, I mean . . . ' She flapped after me.

'Hope you find a nice tenant for it. Thanks again. Bye now.'

I actually turned to leave. And for a moment she let me go, and I thought I'd over-cooked it. Then . . .

'No, no, wait a minute, Mr Shelley.'

'Yes?'

'Well, I mean, I think it would be all right.' She managed a smile again. 'If you like it, that is.'

'Oh well . . .'

'I mean, you know . . .'

I was not about to let her off that easily. I hummed and haa'd a bit. I produced my agency list, with its impressive addresses. And come to think of it, I wasn't going to commit myself there and then. Why not? Well, you'll come to know Fran better as we go along, and then you'll understand. She's a lady who likes to be in on the big decisions. So I stood and thought about this, while Mrs H. stood and hopped from one foot to the other.

'I do have a couple of other places to see, you know . . .'

'Oh yes, of course.'

'Why don't I bring Fran back this evening, 'bout six, give you a chance to think things over?'

'Yeah, awright.' She was happy.

'And you can meet her . . .'

'Of course, yes.'

'And she can meet you.'

'Yes, yes.' She was delighted. I was a lovely man.

'I mean,' I told her, 'I wouldn't want to pressure you in *any* way.'

'No, no.' I got her best and most grateful smile. Perhaps she wasn't quite as sharp as I'd assumed. 'That's very nice of you.'

'Not at all. See you about six then.'

'Yeah.' She sketched a little wave with her hand.

I went to the top of the stairs, then turned back.

'Oh, and take my word for it.'

'What?'

'There's nothing wrong with that moulding.'

Coming up – Nasty Experience of the Day, Number Two. It happened in the next flat.

I thought I ought to keep looking. I wished I hadn't.

Mr Patel, the landlord, had clearly modelled his accommodation on the Black Hole of Calcutta. It was a disgrace, a tip, and a slum. All right, I'm prejudiced. I don't like landlords. Mr Patel was the sort who gave them a bad name.

He showed me the door to the room. I opened it. Peered in. Then closed it, with all due reverence.

'Don't tell me – your great-great-grandmother died in here, and it hasn't been touched since.'

Patel laughed like a blocked drain. 'Ha-ha-ha. You very funny man. Please go in.'

'Shouldn't we send a canary in first?'

He didn't get that one. 'Please?'

I opened the door again. Cautiously. Nothing actually ran out and bit me. I think something stirred in a dark corner, I wasn't sure.

'No, it must be all right,' I told Patel. 'The rats look healthy enough. What was this place? A reject depot for Oxfam shops?'

We entered the room. For a moment I thought it was well carpeted. Then I realised that the pile beneath my feet was a pile of muck.

'I show you everything,' said India's Answer to Rachmann. 'This is making hot water.'

'This' was a sort of Bronze age geyser.

'I saw one once in the Science Museum,' I told him.

'I'm sorry?'

I looked around as my eyes became accustomed to the gloom. It was horrid. The curtains were grey winding sheets. Thc bed was a medieval mantrap. The wardrobe undoubtedly a coffin. Dirt clung to the walls. The place was squalid.

I told Patel straight, 'This place is squalid.'

'No, no.' He was quite hurt. 'It is needing only smartening up. I don't mind if you decorate it.'

'What with? Cave paintings?' I tried. But my guide was moving on.

'This is the cooker.'

It was a Baby Belling. Now the reason you find Baby

Bellings in ancient flats is, Belling make 'em to last. But this one had survived beyond the limits of decency. I think it was held together with string.

'Fanny Craddock used to live here, did she?'

'What?'

'Look,' I told him, 'I don't want to waste your time, you've probably got a lot more tombs to open, I'll just . . .'

'You don't want to live here?' A little slow on the uptake, Mr Patel.

'I wouldn't let a pig live here, mate.'

White teeth gleamed in the gloom. 'Please, no pigs, it is not right for my religion.'

I was beginning to become irritated. 'How can letting a room like this be right for any religion? What are you? A Satanist?'

'I was only making the joke.'

Annoyed, I kicked the mantrap. 'Look at this heap of refuse.'

'This is the bed,' Patel claimed. 'Sheets provided.'

'Ah, sheets. I thought for a minute it was the mummy's shroud.' I lifted one of the grey bits of cloth, and looked. Ooooh. Talk about 'All Creatures Great And Small'.

'What poor sod was desperate enough to live here?' I asked. 'Lord Lucan?'

Then I sniffed. That was a mistake. Waves of something awful flooded the old nasal passages. 'I mean, what's the smell in this house?'

Patel was pleased to explain. 'This is only today. The man downstairs has brought some work home.'

'What is he? A grave robber?'

'No, no, he's making photographs. It is the chemicals only. I will talk to him.'

I walked to the door, turned, looked at the wretched man in his wretched room. 'Mr Patel, I've seen a lot of places today, but I think, on balance, this is the worst.'

'Oh, no.'

'Competition has been fierce,' I agreed. 'But I think that here you've actually achieved uninhabitability.'

'It is very cheap, this room.'

'I wouldn't take this room if it included a pension and a supply of naked women.'

Patel brightened. 'Oh yes. Any women you like to stay here. I have no morals.'

Well. He was right there.

THREE

I SETTLED for Mrs H.

I might have gone on hacking around those seedy flophouses, tripping over frayed stair-carpets, jiggling broken light-switches, disturbing colonies of black-beetles behind cookers, wondering what the stain in the bath really was, and listening to the batty babbling of lunatic landlords who seem to believe that some people actually like living in dirt and desolation.

But I settled for Mrs H.

After all, I told myself as I slopped back into that morning's café, and prepared myself for another cup of their hot grey water, Mrs H.'s flatlet was okay. Not that it had many advantages. The important thing was, it had none of the usual disadvantages. It was clean. It was sound of construction, reasonably furnished, and private. One could actually imagine living in it for more than two days without going doolally-tap, as my mother says when she forgets herself.

What's more, there was Mrs H. Not, I agreed with myself, one of nature's loveliest ladies, but she had one great redeeming feature – she liked and trusted me. I had won her approval. Or, to put it another way, she'd been conned.

'Coffee, please. Medium roast Columbian.'

Rather a provocative order, I agree. But the waitress – the same one as at our morning session – didn't object. Indeed, she looked down at me, over those great swelling mounds of overall, and there was a gleam in her eye that had not been there that morning. Something . . . secretive! And exciting. She licked her lips.

'You was 'aving a go at me.'

'What?'

'Trolleyism. I found out what it means.'

'Really, well . . . '

Oh dear! She must have looked it up. I should have got in first, and told her that 'trolleyism' was having it away in a Sainsbury's wire basket. Too late now . . .

'It's with three, innit?' She grinned, and then said, with undoubted admiration, 'Dirty sod.'

'Well, it's not necessarily . . . ' I tried.

'Nuffin' to do with sossage toad.'

'It *is* a tenuous connection,' I agreed. 'Diagrammatic rather than actual.'

'Is that another dirty word?'

She should have been annoyed with me, but she wasn't. That gleam was still in her eye. And now, instead of stalking off in a huff to lukewarm-up my coffee, she leaned across the table and adjusted the position of the red plastic sauce 'tomato'. In doing so she managed to bring her cleavage to within two inches of my nose. A mixture of Johnson's Baby Powder and Tramp floated up from the opening, contrasting rather strongly with whatever was emanating from the plastic sauce tomato. Then she straightened up again, while I tried to uncross my eyes.

'You know, you're wasted here,' I told her. 'A girl with your talents could be shifting plasterboard by the truckload.'

'What?'

'You going to get my coffee today or tomorrow?'

Still no sign of her taking offence. Instead she said, 'Anna Raeburn goes on about men like you.'

I wanted to say, 'Good – 'cos I go on about women like Anna Raeburn,' but I felt that those waters would run too deep, and instead I said, 'I've never met the woman.'

To which she said, 'You think sex is dirty, don't you?'

Which in turn gave me the punch line: 'With luck, if you work at it.'

Much more of this, and we'd be a double act.

Except that this Madonna of the Coffee Machine wasn't joking. Tentatively she said, 'See, maybe you're right, I dunno . . .'

Right about what?

She sat down on the chair next to me. Nylon overall brushed casually against denim jean. We were suddenly no longer customer and waitress, we were a feller and a bird. Things were getting out of hand.

'Was that your girlfriend you was with?'

Oh boy! She thinks Fran and me would like her to . . . 'Don't sit too close,' I warned. 'My after-shave may rob you of your reason.'

She didn't need a reason. She just leaned closer. 'Only I was quite interested in what you was saying. See . . .'

I held up a magisterial hand. This had got to stop. I've nothing against people going to bed together, in threes, fours, or multiples thereof. What I had to worry about was the problem of explaining to Fran how the subject ever arose in the first place. I had to talk my way out of this, and quickly. I chose the simple method.

'Before you go any further – what's your star sign?'

It never fails, this astrology junk. You can con your way in and out of every possible situation simply by mentioning star signs. Don't bother to learn any of the mumbo-jumbo. Make it up as you go along. It always works. At least it has always worked for me.

'Gemini,' said the waitress.

I pulled a face that would have made Scrooge look cheerful. 'Ah. Well. I'm afraid we're doomed from the start.' She looked sad, and I added – with more hope than expectation – 'I'd run off and get my coffee if I was you.'

'What are you then?' she asked.

'Cancer.' I always say that, it sounds dangerous. 'We like our coffee strong,' I added, motive as above.

'What's your girlfriend?'

Heaven knows. 'Libra,' I guessed.

The waitress pulled a face. 'Oh, I don't like Libras. They're creepy.'

'Nice of you to say so, I'll pass that on to Fran.'

She smiled. Perhaps she thought she was being nice. 'They're all arty. Paintin' and writin' and that.'

'Gemini are frank and forthcoming, are they?'

'Oh no! We're shy and withdrawn.' And she began to demonstrate her shyness and withdrawal by picking up the plastic sauce tomato and wiping it with a cloth. The fabulous chest began to bounce again.

'But we've got loving and loyal natures,' she went on. 'What do you do for a living?'

I blinked a little at the non-sequitur, but managed a reply. 'I'm a freelance layabout. We have idle and lazy natures. I'm thinking of chucking it, though. The competition's too fierce these days.' I tried a non-sequitur of my own. 'You've nearly wiped the bloom off that tomato.'

She inspected the thing. 'We have to keep them clean. All the sauce runs down the side.'

That sounded suspiciously like a philosophy of life, and I wanted to say so, but I thought it might bring her back to sex. I tried another tack.

I held up the plastic tomato. 'They're an emblem of our generation, these things, you know. No other age could have produced that. I mean, you can't see one of those nestling between the Adam candlesticks on a Chippendale sideboard, can you? Or being passed down the table at the Last Supper. No, this is a genuine artifact – the Sixties' Tomato. Their exuberance of form and colour an embarrassment in the austere seventies, an insult in the painful eighties. People will collect these in years to come, you know. Sotheby's will auction them by the truss.'

She listened to all this as if she understood, and then demonstrated that she didn't. 'I suppose they are good.'

'I once wrote "I love you" in ketchup all over Mary Hamilton's chips with one of these,' I remembered. 'We Cancers are given to flamboyant gestures.'

'Who's Mary Hamilton?'

I heaved a Barbara Cartland-type sigh. 'The first of many women to whom I wished to devote my life. I was thirteen at the time. Unfortunately her life was devoted to chips, and she noticed neither the message nor its author. She married a potato farmer, and died of obesity in 1974.'

The bosom swelled with the drama of it all. 'She didn't!'

'No,' I grinned, 'but I like my stories to have happy endings.'

She grinned back. It made me feel uneasy. We were getting intimate again. Danger.

'Tell me,' I said brusquely, 'do people always have to talk to you for half an hour to get a cup of coffee, or is the after-shave belatedly coming in to its own?'

She sniffed, and stood up. 'I'll go and get it. I've only got one pair of hands, you know.'

And she went. Which was just as well, because the door swung open, and in came Fran.

She came striding towards me across the café, and it became one of those moments when I realise exactly why I turn down my chances with other women. Her hair was flowing long and loose, and her eyes were shining straight into mine, and she looked as if I was the only person in the world she could ever want. I suppose that's why I felt the same about her. She dumped herself down opposite me, and for a moment we just grinned at each other, in the sheer pleasure of being there together. Daft, aren't we!

Then her expression changed, to one of more basic pleasure. 'Shelley,' she announced, 'I've got somewhere.'

'Yeah?'

'Bed-sit and kitchen.'

Coincidence. 'So've I,' I told her. 'Where?'

'Pangloss Avenue.' Somehow she made it sound desirable. 'Just round here. I got it from that agency.'

I sighed. 'Not Mrs Hawkins?'

'Yes.' Eyes big and round. 'How do you know?'

'I got it as well.' Was Mrs H. planning a commune?

'No, you didn't.' Fran dug in her handbag, and produced two of Mr Yale's products on a ring.

'You got the keys?' I asked stupidly.

'Paid two week's rent!'

'But . . . ' I began to have that queasy feeling in the gut, a feeling which means something's going on that I ought to know about, but don't.

'Shelley, I had to. Couldn't risk losing it. I've left a bag, so we can't be got out now.' Clever girl, my Fran.

'The room on the first floor?'

'Yeah.'

'I don't understand.' An understatement. 'She's keeping that room for me. I'm to go back at six to show it to you.'

'Nice, isn't it!'

'It'll do,' I agreed. 'I've been trying all day to do better.'

'No luck?'

'No . . . ' I said absently, still trying to work it out. 'A few Paleolithic bed-sits. A Hammer film set in Willesden.' Then a thought struck me. 'Did you tell her about me?'

'I never tell people about you.' Fran enjoyed that one, and giggled to herself.

I sensed trouble. Something had Gone Wrong, in capitals. That nasty feeling in the tum was getting worse. I must have been sussed. Mrs H. – who I thought loved and trusted me – had ditched me. Why? Had someone been going around spreading nasty truths about me?

'I think we ought to get round there,' I said urgently.

'Have you eaten?'

'No.'

'I'm starving.' Fran rubbed her hands in anticipation of food, and began reading the menu.

'There's something wrong,' I worried.

'Shelley . . . ' Fran did her I'm-Speaking-To-An-Idiot bit. 'We've got the place. We can't be got out.'

'No.' But . . .

'I say!' Fran waved at the waitress, who sailed majestically across to our table, and stood looking at her rather sideways.

Fran smiled at her. 'Could we have some Toad-in-the-hole?'

The waitress dropped her pad. 'Oh don't you start, for God's sake!'

Sometime later we were safe in our new flatlet. Fran was as happy as a pig in clover, growing more housewifey by the minute as she clattered around in the tiny kitchen, making tea. Or coffee. I myself lay in a state of total collapse on the bed, partly through the tension of possibly meeting Mrs H. on the stairs when we came in – we didn't – and partly through exhaustion after having to explain things to Fran and the waitress. It had not been easy, I might tell you. And at the end of it all, Fran and the waitress regarded each other with a mutual suspicion which was only exceeded by their mutual suspicion of me. Oh well . . .

Fran came in bearing cups. With her arms held out, and the light behind her, it would have been a dull man who failed to notice the shape of her waist and the swing of her hips. I am not dull. Certain automatic relays began to click within my personal computer. I patted the place on the bed beside me.

'Nice bed.' Amazing the implication one can put into two simple words.

Fran gave me that old-fashioned look that never goes out of fashion. She gave me my tea, then sat on the floor by the bed.

She looked around. 'We going to do this place up, Shelley?'

I looked around, thought, gave her my considered opinion. 'Um.'

'Well, we're likely to be here for a bit,' she reasoned. 'At least until I'm a rich and successful writer, or you're prepared to soil your hands with honest toil. Equally remote possibilities, I should think. There's a do-it-yourself shop on the corner,' she laughed. 'You could get the gear and renew your acquaintance with Sandra Ferguson at the same time.'

I waved a hand dismissively. 'I've gone off her. I've been stirred by memories of Mary Hamilton since then.'

'Who's she?'

'A simple-minded chip freak to whom I once declared myself in letters of blood.'

The nice thing about Fran is, that sort of thing doesn't throw her. She doesn't want to know chapter and verse. She doesn't even want to know what I'm talking about. She goes along with my little ways. Aren't I lucky?

Now she said, 'I hope I'm the exception among your women.'

'Oh you are. All the others were lookers.' I reached down to her. 'Give us a kiss to be going on with.'

She gave me a kiss to be going on with. And I knew exactly

what that kiss was going on to. I drew her up on to the bed beside me. It wasn't exactly a struggle. That's another nice thing about Fran.

'Shelley . . .'

I kissed her again.

'Shelley, Mrs Hawkins will be up in a minute.'

'Well, she'll have to wait her turn. I can only manage one at a time.'

She giggled. 'That's not what you told that waitress . . . ' and that was the last thing she'd have said for a while if there hadn't been an insistent knock on the door.

She pushed me away gently. 'There you are, what did I tell you?'

I closed my eyes and lay back on the bed. If I'd got up, I'd have fallen over myself. I heard Fran pad across to the door and open it. The voice was familiar enough . . .

'Everything all right then, is it, Frances?'

'Fine, Mrs H.,' said Fran. And then, inevitably, 'Come and meet . . . '

Into the room, and into my line of vision, came Mrs H. I swung my legs off the bed, sat up, and grinned at her. She did not grin back.

'What the 'ell are you doing 'ere?' she screeched instead.

I gestured to Fran. 'This is the lady who's not my wife, Mrs Hawkins.'

She didn't mess about, not Mrs H. 'You can bugger off out of it!'

Fran said calmly, 'This is my boyfriend, Mrs Hawkins.'

' 'Im? It's all off!'

'What?' from Fran.

'You're a bleeding con man, you are!' Mrs H. told me, and her voice rang with understandable conviction.

'I'm sorry?'

'I phoned the Labour about you. Asked them for a reference.'

She did *what*? 'You did *what*?'

'I know all about you.'

I shook my head. 'They'd never tell you . . .'

'I spoke to a Mr Alan Forsyth.'

'Ah.' That explained a lot. Everything in fact. Vindictive old sod Forsyth. Clever old boot Mrs H.

'Told me all about you,' she went on. 'Everything. He was very 'elpful.'

Fran decided to be helpful. 'Mrs Hawkins . . .'

Mrs H. overrode her. 'And the do-it-yourself shop on the corner 'as never heard of polydrops aggravated glue.'

'What?' from Fran again . . . I reminded myself to tell her about charging rhinos at forty paces later on.

' 'E was cracking on the house was falling down, and 'e could fix it,' Mrs H. told her. 'Told me 'e was a 'ouse restorer.'

I got to my feet and tried to look penitent. 'I do apologise, Mrs H. You see, I'm a compulsive liar.'

'No, you're not, Shelley,' Fran remonstrated. 'Don't tell lies.'

I sensed that the conversation was slipping out of control.

'Telling me your mother was dead,' Mrs H. said grimly.

'Dead?' Fran looked at me, then back at Mrs H. 'She's skiing, Mrs Hawkins.'

'Don't you start!' Mrs Hawkins squawked.

'In Scotland,' Fran insisted.

'Oh, no she isn't!'

Fran looked at her, bewildered. 'She *is*, Mrs H.'

Mrs H. delivered her clincher. 'Ow can she go skiing? With a wooden leg?'

Fran said 'What?' for the third time in so many minutes.

'Well, I'm sorry, love,' Mrs H. went on with finality, 'burrit's all off. I'm not 'aving no bleeding useless layabouts in this 'ouse.'

I decided to take a hand in all this. I stood up straight, then walked in the most formidable way I know towards Mrs H. She didn't give an inch.

'I'm very sorry, Mrs Hawkins,' I said with metallic clarity, 'but if you're going to be rude I'm afraid I shall have to ask you to leave our room.'

She didn't give a centimetre. 'For your information, Mr 'Igh and Mighty, this does 'appen to be my 'ouse.'

'But we've taken possession of this bit, you see,' I pointed out.

'What?'

'You've issued keys,' I reminded her.

'Eh?'

I rubbed it in. 'And accepted rent.'

'That's right, Mrs Hawkins,' Fran said more gently. 'We've moved in.'

'Oh, no you 'aven't!' She tried hard, but now she lacked conviction.

I spread my arms wide. 'Demonstrably we have, Mrs Hawkins.'

There was a long and significant silence. I found my tea cup, raised it, sipped noisily.

And then, to my vast pleasure, Mrs H. departed, leaving behind a cliché of quite titanic proportions.

'You 'aven't 'eard the last of this!'

She slammed the door behind her. The moulding in the corner of the ceiling fell heavily and messily to the floor. The first battle was won. The war would doubtless continue. I sipped again.

'Fran?'

'What?'

'Is this tea or coffee?'

Then I ducked. Quickly.

FOUR

BY HEAVEN, the layabout's life can be a lonely one! People don't know, people don't care, how we who do nothing suffer. You don't care, do you? *Do* you? Be honest, have you ever given a single moment's thought to the problems a layabout faces when he contemplates another entire day of idleness? To how he may fill those long tedious hours between nine and five? No, of course you haven't. Nothing has ever been done for us. Nothing ever will be done for us. We remain for ever alone. And . . . lonely!

This particular day is a case in point. It is another Thursday, some few weeks after Fran and I had decided to live, laugh and love together about three feet above Mrs Hawkins's head. Things had not gone too smoothly between landlord and tenant, but more of them anon. Meanwhile, picture me on this Thursday morning, suffering all the mental and physical pain of my chosen profession – unemployment. I am idle, and alone.

Well . . . almost alone. There is Maggie.

Maggie is a lovely girl. She has a lovely chest. It is not exactly on the same scale as the superstructure fronting the waitress in the café. But it has a beauty all of its own. Let me put it like this: if the bosom of the waitress is a juggernaut lorry, then that of Maggie is a Lotus. Yes, a high-speed super GT something-injected formula-whatever Lotus. Lovely to look at – and very much out of my reach!

Maggie is out of my reach for two good reasons. Firstly, she is engaged to be married to someone who works for a living and owns at least two suits. Secondly, she stands safely on the other side of a large, polished bit of wood commonly known as a 'bar'. It is, in fact, the bar in the 'Snug' of The Ship. Maggie and I are there, in the Snug, alone. But the bar comes between us. Now I know there are men who, if they were there alone with Maggie, would take three great strides across the lino, vault the bar, and sweep her into their arms. But I'm not like that. And anyway, at that time of the day – about twelve – the men who do that sort of stuff are off doing other manly things, like checking VAT accounts or selling double-glazing. So even though we are alone and unobserved, Maggie is safe behind her bar. I am content to squat on a stool, watch her over the rim of a pint, and think lustful thoughts.

However, I am not happy. For one thing it's too quiet. For another, it will soon be lunch time, and all the office workers will come clambering in, and then it will be too noisy. It's never right. And at this time in the morning beer never tastes like it did the night before.

That, then, is how things were on this particular morning. I was not happy. And perhaps it showed.

Maggie bent forward solicitously between the beer taps. 'What's wrong, Shelley?'

She caught me in mid-experiment. To amuse myself I had invented a little game. I had stared fixedly at Maggie's front, and then gradually I had allowed my eyes to cross. Yes, it worked! I could now see *four* of 'em! If I could patent it, I'd be rich. However, life is never that generous. I soon realised the snag. What I gained in quantity, I lost in definition. Oh well. Then Maggie spoke, and I slowly let my eyes return to normal. I felt a bit dizzy.

'What's wrong, Shelley?' she said again.

'Life.'

'Yeah, I know what you mean.'

I was glad she knew what I meant. I'm sure I didn't. I'm sure you don't. But Maggie is an understanding girl.

'That and not being able to have your body,' I added.

She giggled. 'Shelley, you are awful.'

'I can't help it, love,' I explained. 'I'm as randy as a rabbit. I'm dragged through each day by my frantically twitching loins. It's like Rod Hull and Emu. I'm always frightened my emu'll run off on its own, and cause havoc.'

As I produced this picturesque simile, I began to have doubts about it. After all, Emu has got a dirty great arm stuffed up him. However . . .

Maggie pulled a face. 'You wouldn't be unfaithful to Fran in a million years.'

'No, I suppose not.' I finished the last of my pint. It was beginning to taste a little better. Time must be getting on. 'Want a drink?' I asked her.

'Oh, ta.' She pulled herself a half, sensible girl. 'Same again?'

'Yeah.'

She took my glass, and once more heaved on the old beer tap. Muscles swelled. Tendons tightened. Valleys deepened. Mountains peaked . . .

'My God you're a well-built girl,' I told her. 'Look at that chest.'

'Do you mind?' Maggie was used to this.

'I haven't seen a pair like that since I was in Ordnance Survey.' That got a smile. 'When's your happy day?' I asked.

'I like the way your mind works. June the fourteenth.'

'He's a lucky man,' I said, meaning it.

'So I tell him, only he won't listen.'

'No. A male weakness, that.'

'What is?'

'Being hard-of-hearing. All to do with long solitary adolescences. So I'm told.'

Well, that was what my mate at school reckoned. Doing it made you deaf. Another school of thought maintained that it sent you blind. Yet another insisted that it would cause it to drop off. And then there were the 'hair-on-the-palm-of-the-hand' brigade, and . . . well, what did it matter? We all did it, even the ones who were good at rugger. *Especially* the ones who were good at rugger.

There was a crash off-stage. I jumped, then remembered that the pub had got the builders in, and they were busy destroying some rather attractive wooden screening in the saloon bar.

'What are they doing to this place?' I asked Maggie.

'Oh it's all being improved, they've nearly finished. It's going to be re-named The Victory, and everything's going to be changed.'

My heart sank. 'How changed?'

'Well, this bar's going to be The Foc's'le,' Maggie explained with enthusiasm. 'The public's going to be The England Expects – and guess what they're going to have on the Gents' door?'

I sighed. 'As long as it isn't "Kiss Me, Hardy", I really don't care.'

'No, silly. Horatio's. And Lady Hamilton's for the Ladies'.'

'The ultimate accolade.' What puerile nonsense was this, I wondered? The place was a pub, not a pantomime. Whatever next?

'And we're all going to wear sailor suits.'

'Oh, my God!' No more, please . . .

'And instead of wall-paper there's going to be wooden planking.'

'And instead of beer,' I said, taking up the refrain, 'there's going to be bilge-water.'

Maggie shook her head seriously. 'No. It's going to be all keg.'

'That's what I said.'

My worst fears had been confirmed. Yo-ho-ho and a half-pint of fizz. Aloud, I said, 'Dear God, another heap of plastic kitsch.'

'What's wrong with it being like a ship?'

'What's wrong with it being like a pub?' I exploded. 'When Nelson fought the Battle of Trafalgar it was in a ship, not a plastic replica of The Green Man. What the hell's Nelson got to do with your lunchtime pint?'

Loyal Maggie was offended. 'He was a great man.'

'So what? He's got an appropriate monument.'

Maggie added, '*And* a great lover.'

'Well . . .' I couldn't resist it. 'For a great lover he has a *very* appropriate monument.'

'What?'

'Nothing.' Let her 'lucky man' explain – if he's man enough.

'Oh well . . . ' I took a last big swallow of precious real beer, 'better be off. Fran'll wonder where I've got to.'

'How is she?'

'She feels okay to me,' I said, remembering a rather warm and wonderful cuddle we'd indulged in earlier that morning.

'Shelley . . . ' Maggie wrinkled her pretty face at me.

'What?'

'Why don't you marry her?'

Funny, that's exactly what I'd asked myself after the warm and wonderful cuddle. There was an answer, of course. But I wasn't about to give it to Maggie. Instead . . .

'Can't do that, love. You lose dole that way.' Oh, my God, dole! 'That reminds me – is it Thursday?'

'Yeah.'

'Christ, I got to sign on.'

Maggie tutted. 'You should have gone this morning.' She'll make her man a wonderful nag.

'Yeah, well, I only just got up.'

'Ugh!' She pulled a face. 'How can you drink beer first thing?'

The answer to that one was with practice and perseverance, but I didn't bother.

'Fran's got me lunch on,' I explained instead. 'And I can't eat on an empty stomach. Tra, Mags.'

'Tra.' Maggie gave me a wave and a grin. Her feller is a lucky man, he really is.

Why didn't I marry Fran? Well . . .

'We've only got sardines.'

Now how's that for a greeting from one lover to another? 'We've only got sardines.' If someone's going to say something like that to me as soon as I walk through the door, it ought to be a wife. It's a wifely thing to say. 'We've only got sardines.' Come to think of it, it's a good title for a music-hall song. Like 'Yes, we have no bananas.' 'We've only got sardines, dooby-doo.'

'We've only got sardines.' Fran looked at me expectantly. I had to say something.

'I like sardines, that's why I got them.'

She held out the opened can of tiny fish which I'd put in the fridge. They looked a bit tatty, to be truthful.

'Where did you get them?' she asked.

'I dunno. I picked them up somewhere.'

'Only they're South African . . .'

'What!!'

But I had no time to react to this latest assault on my liberal principles. Someone knocked loudly on the door, and by now I knew exactly who it had to be.

'Enter at your peril, Mrs Hawkins!' I called. 'At this very moment we are writhing in carnal ecstasy on our illicit bed, glorying in the delights of our naked bodies. Yes, Fran, Yes! Oh Fran – Fran! Yes, now!!! Now . . . Aaaaaaaaaaaa-hhhhhhhh . . .'

Mrs Hawkins came right on in.

'You 'aven't given me no rent,' she announced.

I wondered vaguely what the effect on my sexual prowess would have been had Fran and I actually been writhing in carnal ecstasy and so on, only to be interrupted by a face like Mrs Hawkins's and an announcement like the above. Coitus interruptus can be damaging. All right, we all have to cope with the odd phone call, and cats have been known to play chase with my toes at the wrong moment. I know one feller who was a devotee of the up-against-the-kitchen-sink method, and he was interrupted by the oven timer. But the pugnacious 'You 'aven't given me no rent', combining as it did irritation, impertinence, and accuracy, might have put me off the whole activity for good. Or two days. Whichever was the shorter.

Mrs H. knew nothing of these thoughts, and would have cared less if she had known. She stood, her arms in that position which I believe is known as 'akimbo', but I'm not sure, and she waited for a response.

'True, but . . .' I began, and that was enough for her.

'*And* you've broken open the meters again.'

I had a friend at school who told the careers master he

wanted to be a meteorologist because they were so easy to break into.

'A short term loan, I promise—' I began again.

'*And* you've pinched the cat's sardines.'

Oh dear. She'd found that out too. Fran put the can down on the table and gave me a filthy look. Why didn't I marry her? What difference would it make?

'Well, don't worry,' I told Mrs H. 'I'm not going to pinch any more sardines. They're South African.'

'What's wrong with South African?' she wanted to know. 'You prejudiced or something?'

'Prejudiced!' My hackles rose. Then they sank back again. What was the use? Come to that – what are hackles?

Mrs Hawkins sighed. 'Gawd, you're a trial,' she told me. 'Give us some money and shut up, I ain't got nuffin' for Willie's tea.'

It had taken me some days to discover whether the aforesaid 'Willie' was Mrs H.'s husband or Mrs H.'s cat. He had proved, in the end, to be the husband, although, as Fran had discovered during lengthy and intimate chats over the teapot with Mrs H., Willie's husbandly performance was distinctly below that of the cat – *and* the cat had been neutered. 'Willie': a singularly inappropriate name, I mused. However . . .

'Mrs H.,' I said, using my frank voice. 'I am without funds. If it were humanly possible I would, but . . . '

She sank that one without trace. 'You 'ad twenty-three quid off the Security this morning. Fifteen benefit and eight arrears.'

My mouth had dropped open at this, and I tried to shut it inconspicuously. 'How do you know?' I asked.

'I opened your letter.' No trace of shame.

'That's against the law.'

'So's breaking into gas meters.' She held out a washday-red hand. 'Give us ten on account.'

I handed over the cash. There are times when I quite admire Mrs H. And I felt I wanted to express this admiration.

'You,' I told her, 'are a vicious unfeeling capitalist, Mrs H. You property speculators live high on the sufferings of the oppressed classes. Up the revolution.'

'Up you, lover boy!'

See what I mean? Sometimes the old boot has style.

'My Willie worked 'ard to buy this 'ouse,' she continued, 'and now 'e works 'ard to keep it fit for you to live in. And all you do is sit on your lazy bum all day.'

Lazy bum?

'The pampering of my posteriors,' I began, all ready to conduct a detailed examination of the relative athletic qualities of our bodies, with reference to early-morning exercise in that lovely double bed, as compared to Mrs H.'s barely used twin divans, but Mrs H. wasn't having any of it.

'And you can cut out all the lah-di-bloody-da,' she swept on. 'I'll believe in your education and all when you can turn it into 'ard cash.'

A casual witness of this scene might expect that there would now follow a total breakdown in the relationship between Mrs Hawkins and her tenants. But a casual witness would not know Mrs Hawkins, who now turned with a friendly smile to Fran, and asked, 'Got any tea on the go, love?'

She got an equally friendly grin from Fran. 'I'll make some, Mrs H.'

These two had developed a relationship over the weeks that most certainly excluded me. They were, God help us all, friends. They actually got on. It was something that puzzled me, I must admit, because Fran isn't the type of girl who automatically makes friends with other women just because they are women. Fran doesn't need anyone to go to the Ladies' with. And, loath as I am to ascribe good qualities to her, neither does Mrs H. But somehow the two of them had found common ground.

I had a sneaking suspicion that, in some nasty twisted way, this common ground was me.

Anyway, tea was upcoming. Fran went into the kitchen. The common ground ground his teeth. Mrs H. sat down at the table expectantly, and looked around her.

'Gawd, this place looks dreadful,' she remarked.

I sat down opposite and looked at her earnestly, 'You're charging an exorbitant rent for it, Mrs H.'

'The rent is *not* exorbitant.'

'That's not what the rent officer said.'

Then I sat back and waited for the deluge. It came.

'Five pounds we asked for this place,' she began, 'and it was a palace when you moved in. By the time you got the rent-officer round 'ere you'd torn the wall-paper off, stuck 'alf a dozen Tesco mushrooms on the wall, and started a mouse farm. No wonder 'e knocked the rent down to three.'

Was she right? Was what she said true? Well, parts of what she said were true. And all of what she said was partly true. She'd certainly caught the spirit of our recent relationship.

'Mrs H. . . . ' I began, but she hadn't finished.

'And when I complained to the law you done me for victimisation, and when I put mousetraps down you phoned the RSPCA. This 'ouse is like nineteen eighty-bloody-four. If you'd studied at school like you've studied the Rent Act, you'd be a BA.'

But I am a BA, I thought. In English . . . or history . . . well, something like that.

'I am a BA,' I told her.

'BF, more like.'

Fran emerged from the kitchen, grinning at that, and she gave Mrs H. her cuppa.

'Thanks, love.' Mrs H. held her tea and shook her head at me. 'Why on earth you stay with 'im, I'll never know.'

I wasn't hanging about to discuss that. 'I'm off down the dole.'

'You should 'ave gorn this morning,' Mrs H. told me sententiously.

'What about your lunch?' Fran asked.

'I'm not eating apartheid fish!' I thought I'd had the last word. But as I left, I heard Mrs H. get it instead.

'I'll 'ave 'em back for the cat then. 'E's not prejudiced.'

FIVE

'GOOD EVENING, Mr Shelley.'

It wasn't evening, of course. It was scarcely afternoon. Saying 'evening' was the Alan Forsyth method of conveying that I was late signing on again. Irony is not his strong point. Subtlety is not his strong point. His only strong point is the end of his nose.

'You remembered my name,' I remarked.

He gave a jolly laugh. 'I try to keep in with the regular customers. Good for business.'

That rang a bell. It was what *I* had told *him*. Well, perhaps he was learning.

'You should have been here this morning,' he added.

'So I'm told. Yeah. I wasn't feeling too well.'

'I'm sorry to hear that.' He looked about as sorry as a cat on a radiator. 'What was it? Exhaustion?'

'You're wasted here,' I told him. 'You should be a comedy writer. The matchbox companies are crying out for people like you.'

'You cheeky bugger!' Forsyth was stung to what passes for his quick. 'You're all the same, you people today . . . '

Hello! I'd never got him going like this before. His nasty little face was glowing pink with rage, and he was rocking back and forth as he spoke . . .

'You're all the same, you people today, you make me sick. If I had my way—'

'We'd have National Service, short hair, and we'd call you sir,' I put in. 'And do you know what else we'd have?'

He bought it. 'No?'

'The bloody world war to go with it!' I sighed. Victory over a fool like Forsyth was nothing to write home about. Even if Mrs Hawkins would read the letter.

'Can I just sign my name please?' I asked.

His little eyes gleamed. 'No, you can't. Not yet.'

Warning bells rang deep within my ears. Something, I suspected, was up!

'The Inspector wants a word with you.'

Stone me, something *was* up!

Forsyth pointed a bony finger. 'Cubicle three.' As I went, I could hear him sniggering to himself.

The Inspector was a rather nice-looking man, really – or he would have been if he hadn't been wearing such an obviously respectable and expensive suit. He was shortish and darkish and youngish – obviously a high flyer. Certainly not the sort of middle-aged fascist bully I've met on other similar occasions, nor the frustrated and passed-over failure that Forsyth typifies. One way or the other, I was prepared to give the Inspector a chance to join the human race. So I began as politely as I knew how.

'Hello, Inspector.'

He was behind a desk, reading some extremely boring-looking papers, and he glanced up, slightly surprised. 'Hello?'

I introduced myself. 'I'm Shelley.'

Light dawned. 'Mr James Shelley?'

'That's right, Inspector.'

'Sit down, Mr Shelley.'

'Thanks, Inspector.'

I sat. All well so far. Of course, looked at in retrospect, it couldn't last.

'There's no need to call me "Inspector",' said the Inspector. Then, with his mouth twisted in derision and his voice overloaded with sarcasm, he added, 'This isn't "Z Cars", you know.'

'Ah,' I said.

But I was thinking a great deal more than 'ah'. You see, it isn't always me who starts it, is it? I'd been prepared to conduct the interview along reasonable and sober lines, with courtesy and respect for each individual involved, with honesty and directness, perhaps even with a nice cup of tea and a friendly handshake at the end of it all. But not him. He'd just thrown all that out of the window. Very well, if he wanted it the difficult way he could have it the difficult way. Let no quarter be asked, let no quarter be given. And when it's over, let's all remember who started it.

'You should have been here this morning,' the Inspector told me. I think that made him the fourth person to remind me of the fact.

'Really?' I said, surprised.

'Yes.'

'Good Lord. Could've sworn it was this afternoon.' I shook my head at the forgetfulness of the human mind.

'Do try and be punctual. It does help us. Now, we're a bit worried about you at Central Office . . .'

I held up a hand to stop him. 'No need, I feel fine.'

' . . . and they've asked me to see if I can help in any way,' he continued, ignoring my interruption with considerable skill, I thought.

I gave him a bright smile. 'Really? Well, yeah, since you ask, I could do with a bit more money. You see . . . '

He held the hand up this time. 'It was more in the way of getting you a job, Mr Shelley.'

'Ah, well, now . . . '

He cleared his throat and tried a new approach. 'What kind of work do you do?'

I sighed with relief. For a few moments there I'd been afraid that the good old D of E had come up with a bright bod for a change. Someone who could ask clever questions. But no, this was the same old garbage. It posed no threat. I relaxed and gave the Inspector an honest answer to his question.

'None. I'm unemployed.'

He flinched. 'I gathered that, Mr Shelley. I mean, what do you usually do?'

'Nothing. I'm usually unemployed. I'm just a layabout.'

He flinched again. I hoped he wasn't going to go to pieces too soon. I was beginning to enjoy myself.

The Inspector straightened his already straight tie, and gave me a warm smile, as designated in section 17 of the Department of Employment training manual for Inspectors.

'Mr Shelley,' he said warmly, 'there's nothing to be ashamed of in being out of work . . .'

I smiled back. 'No, I know.'

'Good.' He wasn't pleased.

'On the contrary,' I suggested.

'Um . . . quite so.' He fiddled with a pencil. 'So . . . what sort of work do you do?'

'I told you. None.'

'I see.' He didn't. Or rather, he did, but he couldn't quite believe it yet. 'Well – what sort of work would you like to do?'

'None. I don't like work.'

The pencil broke in his fingers. 'I mean, for a living.'

I shrugged and smiled. 'I manage.'

He pounced. 'How?'

'On the Security.'

'But that's not much, is it?'

I smiled, as if we had mutually arrived at a satisfactory conclusion. 'That's what I said. I need some more.'

'Look, Mr Shelley . . .' He stopped. The man was confused.

Now here's an important point, which I'd like you to take special note of, if you plan to take up cudgels against authority and so forth. When you've got 'em groggy and leaning on the ropes, as was the position of the Inspector at this moment, you must not be tempted to feel sorry for 'em. If you feel sorry you will make a joke, or say something nice. And then they will get back up off the ropes, and clobber you for your kindness. Instead, develop the killer instinct. Get in there, lad, and finish 'em off!

'At least a threshold payment,' I urged. 'I mean, I'm worth it. I'm an experienced layabout. I could shirk for England over any length.'

'Mr Shelley . . .' His voice had become strangely high-pitched and squeaky, and he stopped, cleared his throat, then tried again.

'Mr Shelley, please try to be serious. The State will not support you indefinitely, you know.'

I knew. 'I had my suspicions. I've never trusted the State.'

He took a form from his desk as he looked at me, and began unthinkingly to fold it into the shape of a paper airplane. Then he realised what he was doing, screwed the paper up, realised that this wasn't the right thing to do either, smoothed it out again, and finally put the thing away in a desk drawer. I smiled at him. He found another form, and a second pencil, and wrote down my name and address again.

'Your qualifications, Mr Shelley – any O-levels?'

'Twelve.'

Sorry about that. And about the details now to come. I'm not boasting. I have a knack for attaining qualifications. I can pass exams like a Methodist minister passes pubs. Or like people in pubs pass water.

'A-levels?' he asked, quite clearly wishing he didn't have to.

'Six.'

'Why didn't you go to university?'

'I did.'

He tensed. 'And got a BA, I suppose?'

I nodded. 'And a PhD.'

'Good God.' His day was finally ruined.

'Does that mean I get more money?' I asked, ready to duck if he became violent.

He did become violent. He broke his second pencil. He found a third. Then he sighed.

'What did you study?'

Thank heaven I remembered. It wasn't history or English. 'Geography. Physical and political. Hated it.' I added the last comment to make sure he didn't suggest I taught the silly subject.

This meant he had to ask the next question, and of course I was ready for it.

'Well, what does interest you?'

'Sex, actually. Now if there was a job . . .'

'Mr Shelley! I am trying to help you!' He realised he was shouting. It seemed very quiet outside the cubicle. I could almost see Forsyth's ear at the keyhole.

The Inspector got his voice back down from the ceiling. 'What did you like best at school?'

'Putting my hand up Beryl Wilson's skirt.'

All right, all right, settle down at the back. Don't get too excited. That was not quite the torrid schoolboy experience it sounds. For one thing, Beryl Wilson didn't know why I wanted to put my hand up her skirt, and for another, I wasn't too sure either. But it was fun wanting to do it, and then more fun when I did it. And I think Beryl Wilson found it fun that I wanted to do it, but not so much fun when I actually did it. If you see what I mean.

The Inspector's face was a picture. Abstract art type. Funny, that. He didn't look exasperated, as I would expect. Just completely blank. I wondered if he was going to have a fit.

Instead, very woodenly, he said, 'I do not wish to know about that.'

'Neither did she,' I said with a merry chuckle. 'Story of my life.'

The Inspector prepared to write once more. 'Who was your last employer?'

'*The Faerie Queen.*'

'Mr Shelley!' The third pencil joined the others in bits on the floor.

I held up my hands in protest. 'It's the name of a magazine. I didn't choose the title.'

To be frank, I liked the title of the magazine. It, and the lady assistant editor, were the two things I liked about it.

'In what capacity were you employed?'

'Poet.' True.

'Is that a joke?'

'Not when your name's Shelley, it isn't!' Very true.

One week, I'd lasted. Duties were pleasant, if arduous. By day I wrote poems, trying hard to make them totally incomprehensible and non-rhyming. By night I made the lady assistant editor. I went to sleep during the morning of press day, and the resulting unfinished poem was praised for its 'completeness'. It was this total seriousness about the place and the people that finished me. I laughed in editorial conference, and was fired. Then I laughed in the bed of the lady assistant editor, and had to find a taxi at three in the morning. Oh well . . .

'So you're a poet?' the Inspector verified.

'Not now, I'm not,' I said hastily. 'I retired.'

The Inspector interlocked his fingers and rested them on the desk in front of him. 'Mr Shelley,' he said carefully, 'I cannot enter your usual occupation as "retired poet". Have you done nothing else?'

'No, well, you haven't got to accept work outside your profession, have you?' Barrack-room lawyer Shelley. 'That's the rule.'

'You mean, you've never done any work at all . . .' His voice was going up the register again.

'I did pack beans once for a while.'

'Aha!' The Inspector unlaced his fingers, and then joined them tip to tip, until he formed an elegant tent shape. 'So you did accept work outside your profession?'

'Oh no!' I was shocked by such an allegation of irregularity. 'This was before I was a poet!'

He had to ask. 'What were you then?'

'When?'

'When you packed beans.'

'I was a bean packer.'

The tent collapsed in the wind.

'You're trying to be clever, laddie.'

Laddie? He was possibly two years older than me. Laddie? 'No, I'm not, Inspector.'

Stalemate.

He thought it was time for the sincere appeal. 'Why won't you be a bit more co-operative?'

I replied in the same earnest tone, 'I don't like the system, you see.'

His voice was thick with reasonableness. 'It's the system that's paying you enough to live on, laddie.'

'You don't like that, do you?'

'No, I don't.'

'So you don't like the system either?'

I thought for a moment he was going to cry. But it's like me old mum used to say, you shouldn't play with the big boys if you can't keep up.

After a lengthy pause, the Inspector cleared his throat, then read aloud all he had written on his form.

'James Shelley. Single. 14 Pangloss Avenue, NW6. No usual occupation.'

I winked. 'That's me!'

Ultra-formal now. 'I shall put my report in, Mr Shelley. I think it is only fair to warn you that we are unlikely to support an able-bodied man of your age for much longer.'

And that was it. They always win in the end. The game is to see how far you can keep them going. But in the end they always win. Ah well . . .

I stood. 'Goodbye, Inspector.'

But he wasn't quite finished. And now, for the first time in the whole interview, he surprised me.

'Did you go to Bell Street School, Mr Shelley?'

What on earth . . . ? 'Yes. How did you know?'

'My wife went there.'

'Really? What was her name?' But I think I already knew.

'Beryl Wilson.'

I left, wondering whether Beryl let the Inspector put his hand up her skirt these days.

When I got home she was still there. Mrs H., that is, not Beryl Wilson. Worst luck. Mrs H. was still drinking my tea. Why didn't she go the whole hog, and have tannin injected intravenously?

'Have another cup, Mrs H.?' I invited. It was weak, but the best I could do. I'd had enough for one day. I needed rest and relaxation.

'Gawd,' said Mrs H., brightening at the sight of my face, 'you look miserable. What's the matter, got a job?'

Fran was concerned, too. 'Something wrong, love?'

I shrugged, and sat down heavily. 'Just hassle. The Social Security would prefer me to be sixty-five and/or disabled.'

There was a brief pause, and then I heard Mrs Hawkins draw in her breath sharply. Oh boy – I was for it!

'Just who do you think you are?' she began.

'Pardon?'

'For your information, Mr 'Ard-Done-By, the rest of us 'umble beings 'as to work for a living. An' if we was all like you there wouldn't be no 'andouts, you know. It makes me wild. My Willie works all the 'ours Gawd sends so 'e can make up enough overtime just to keep 'is 'ead above water. And when 'e does come 'ome all 'e's fit for 'is bed. And I don't mean that like you do. Worse luck. And all for what, I should like to know.'

'So should I, Mrs H.' I meant it. She'd put her finger on the entire problem.

'Not to send useless bloody layabouts to uni-bloody-versity and then keep them in the lap of luxury for the rest of their lives, that's not for what,' Mrs Hawkins went on rather vaguely. Then, 'What did you study at that college?'

'Um . . .' I'd forgotten again.

'There's gorrer be something you're good at apart from getting money out of the State.'

'Geography,' I remembered.

'There you are then.' My head was beginning to ache. I hoped she would finish soon. Fortunately she did. 'Why don't you become a geographist? 'Stead of just laying about? Eh? You make me sick.'

'More tea, Mrs H.?' There was a steely note in Fran's voice, and I think Mrs H. picked it up.

'No, thanks.' She got to her feet. '*I've* got work to do.'

Slam.

I turned to Fran, looking for comfort and sympathy. I found something very different indeed.

'Shelley . . .'

'What?'

'I'm pregnant.'

It had been a difficult day in more than one way. I was tired. I might soon be chucked off the dole. I never react well to surprises.

Those are my excuses. Excuses for what I now said to Fran.

'Would that be my fault?'

Bless her, Fran didn't see what I meant at first. 'No, it's mine, I forgot to take the damned . . .'

And then it clicked. 'Of course it's your bloody fault! What do you *mean*?'

SIX

I'M NOT very fond of humble-pie. It gives me indigestion. So does eating my own words. But I chewed on a couple of Rennies and got on with it.

First I had to make things right with Fran. Not easy, because Fran, like any other woman breaking news of pregnancy to her boyfriend, was rather emotional about it. Being virtually accused of infidelity hadn't helped. But by degrees I won my way back into her favours. 'I'm really sorry, darling' stopped her short of actually biffing me one. 'You know I didn't mean it' produced a glimmer of a smile. 'You know I love you' got my chair up close to hers, and 'Very very much' led to my arm around her shoulders. From then one we progressed rather rapidly, with 'I'll never love anyone else' closely followed by 'You're wonderful', 'You don't know what you do to me', 'Let's get comfortable on the bed', 'Hang on, my trousers are stuck', and eventually 'Aaaaaaahhhhhh.'

Wonderful thing, the English language.

Not long afterwards it was trousers-on time, and I left a happily dozing Fran in the flat while I headed back towards the Department of Employment for some less promising recantation. Suddenly the actual title of the place – Department of *Employment* – had become so much more meaningful.

I went through the graffiti-ridden entrance, and stopped just inside. Forsyth was behind his counter. No other customers. Forsyth was gazing into the middle distance, and thoughtfully cleaning his right ear with a matchstick. So this was work. It looked pretty easy to me.

He saw me, jumped, and nearly pierced an eardrum.

'You still here, Mr Shelley? I thought you'd gone.'

Humble-pie time, I reminded myself. No clever cracks please. Just play it straight, Shelley.

'Yes, I had gone,' I told him. 'I've come back.'

He looked quite concerned for a moment. 'No point in that, mate. You won't get any more money.' He was about as concerned as a wood-louse.

'No, er . . . ' Come on, Shelley. Eat up your humble-pie. Don't *like* humble-pie. Eat it!!

Forsyth smiled like a turnip-lantern. 'No, you better pop off home,' he advised. 'Put your feet up. You've had a hard day.'

'Actually . . . ' This now hurt, physically. 'Actually, I wondered if you could help me.'

'Only too delighted.' Forsyth made a kind of courtly bow over his counter. 'What would you like me to do? Call you a cab?'

'I'd like you to get me a job, actually.'

There, I'd said it. I'd actually got it out. I had sought employment. I was surprised to find that I did not faint. I did not break out into a cold sweat. I was not visited by a plague of boils. Nothing like that happened. In fact, I felt pretty much the same as ever. Disappointing, really.

Not so Forsyth. For him, my words were a genuine belt in the bread-basket. He gasped. He seemed to shrivel. Across his previously expressionless acne ran a look of sheer disbelief. Slowly it changed to one of cynicism, before it disappeared up his left nostril. High on his forehead something twitched.

'What's your game?'

I enjoyed a fleeting but brilliantly clear fantasy of beating Forsyth over the head with a vegetable marrow.

Behind me a door opened. I turned. It was the Inspector from the morning's confrontation. He was intent on reading some juicy item in that week's *Civil Service Gazette*, and he nearly walked into me.

'Inspector!' I called.

He jumped. 'Yes?' Then he recognised me, and his voice fell several octaves on the appreciation scale. 'Oh, it's you, Mr Shelley.'

'Yes. Have you sent in your report, Inspector?'

'No,' he said distantly. 'Not yet. Why?'

I sighed with relief, and heard myself gabbling. 'I just wanted to say I'm sorry about Beryl.'

'What?' He flushed.

'I mean,' I went plunging onwards, 'I didn't get all the way up.'

Sudden silence. It might, I admit, have been phrased better.

'Mr Shelley,' he said with exaggerated patience, 'I really don't think . . .'

'And anyway,' I tried again, 'she was wearing thick, navy-blue—'

'Please, Mr Shelley!'

The Inspector looked as if he could cheerfully strangle me. Forsyth was jiggling up and down with excitement. I made one last attempt to straighten things out about Beryl.

'Well, I suppose she was wearing navy-blue knickers, I didn't get far enough . . . They all did, so I assume . . .'

'MR SHELLEY!'

It was impressive. I don't think I've ever been 'Mr Shelley'd' quite so loudly before. There followed, by contrast, a deathly silence, and it was into this that I dropped my personal bomb-shell for the second time.

'I'm looking for a job.'

Remember Forsyth's reaction – gasps, twitches, cynicism? The Inspector's was a carbon copy.

'What are you up to?' he wanted to know.

I spread my arms wide. 'Well, you see . . . I'm expecting a baby.'

'Mr Shelley,' the Inspector was recovering fast, 'there are no supplementary benefits for pregnant men.'

I took a deep breath. 'My wife's expecting a baby.'

'You're not married,' accused the Inspector. Who trains these people? Mr Pelman?

'No,' I admitted, 'I'm not married, absolutely. Um . . . there is a lady who is expecting a baby.'

'How nice for her,' said Forsyth gratuitously.

'Your baby?' the Inspector asked.

'Yes.' I smiled. Congratulations, I felt, might be in order. None were forthcoming. If Christ had been born in a stable behind a labour exchange, they'd have been in there asking for his birth certificate.

'What's her name?' the Inspector wanted to know.

'Frances Smith.'

Forsyth gave a little crow of delight. 'She signs on here.'

'The Good Shepherd knows his flock,' I intoned.

Forsyth took a step forward and gave me his hard look. 'You do know that it is illegal for a woman who is cohabiting with a man to claim supplementary benefit?'

'Illegal?' Oh Christ, yes, so it is, I've gone and dropped Fran in it. Aloud, 'Yes, it is illegal. Yes. Um . . . we're not actually cohabiting.'

I smiled at them both. The Inspector looked at Forsyth. Forsyth looked at his card-index. I guessed what was coming, and held up a hand to stop him.

'Um . . . we do both live at the same address: 14 Pangloss Avenue . . . err . . .'

'Yes?' asked the Inspector with meaning.

'But . . . in different rooms!'

'In different rooms.' It was not difficult to see that the Inspector didn't believe it.

Forsyth, who was beginning to annoy me even more than the Inspector was, found the whole thing very funny.

'You just popped up one day, and . . . ?'

'Quite so,' I said, to shut him up.

'My word!' the Inspector remarked.

I wondered if his word for it was the same as my word for it. Or whether him and Beryl Blueknickers had a special word for it.

Forsyth wouldn't leave it alone. 'Well, it's understandable, really,' he said with a coarse laugh. 'Both of you with nothing to do all day. Time hangs heavy.'

If he was ready to mix it, so was I.

'I dare say that's how you were conceived,' I told him, 'as a direct result of boredom.'

He poked his face in mine. 'At least I was born in wedlock.'

'Really?' I poked mine back. 'Still, you managed to grow up a right . . . '

'Mr Shelley!' The Inspector prevented a punch-up with his imperious pointing finger. 'Cubicle three please!'

Well, I went into cubicle three again, and the Inspector came too. Thankfully Forsyth didn't. He stayed out at the counter, doing whatever he did in slack moments. Trapping flies in his card-index, I expect. But on the whole he didn't miss much. After some toing and froing, the Inspector told me that despite the power and resources of the great Department of Employment, he had to admit they couldn't find me a job.

'What do you mean, they can't find you a job?'

Fran, looking lovely and extremely non-preggy, was quite hurt that the father of her child should still be denied gainful employment.

'Bad time, they say,' I told her. 'Redundancies and so on.' Not that I could remember them closing any steel works in West Hampstead lately, but that's what they said.

'But . . . ' She still couldn't understand it. Fran had great faith in me, you see. Why weren't ICI and BP fighting for my favours at the front door? She had always assumed that, once I made the traumatic decision actually to earn a crust in the legitimate labour market, I'd be snapped up like Scotch at a bring-a-bottle party.

'But . . . you're more qualified than Kenneth Clark. There must be something.'

I shook my head and explained, 'The bad jobs say I'm too qualified and I won't stay with them. The good jobs say I'm qualified but inexperienced, and why haven't I worked for so long?'

'The in-between jobs?'

'They say inflation has produced a glut of graduates.'

'So say you're not a graduate.'

'Then I'm not qualified for anything.'

Of course it wasn't as simple as that. But it was just as bloody frustrating. There was nothing for me. It grieved me, and it grieved the poor old Inspector down at the Labour Exchange. He was stuck with me.

Useless to point out that if I'd gone straight into a bank from university I would now be a securely employed, cheaply mortgaged, deadly-dull junior under-assistant counter clerk, with no other worries than would I be able to book a squash court for a week next Tuesday.

Futile to suggest that, if I had made the proper approaches to the BBC at the right time, I could, at that moment, be standing in the BBC club sinking Scotch in an effort to get up the courage to go down and be an assistant floor manager on 'That's Life'.

And quite hopeless to imply that if I had taken the right subjects, and gone on to medical school, I could be sitting in my surgery, gazing through the window at my new Rover, and telling some poor benighted housewife that breast cancer is nothing to worry about.

I'd missed my chance of all that. I'd opted out. Stepped off the gravy train.

And now my chances and my choices were both severely limited. A job on the Underground? I wasn't rude enough. A chef for Colonel Saunders? Didn't speak Chinese. Hot dog salesman? Marginally too clean. The list of jobs and disqualifications was endless.

And on top of it all was one simple and undeniable fact – I still didn't really want a bloody job.

But I did want Fran to be happy about the baby. I gave up the glooms about employment, and grinned at her.

'Don't worry,' I said. 'You'll get lots of milk and butter tokens – they look after pregnant women.'

She smiled, and we sat down together on the edge of the bed. I looked at her tummy. 'Five weeks pregnant, eh?' Impossible. Flat as a pancake.

I leaned down and spoke to that familiar part of her lovely body, 'Hello in there, young friend!'

Fran giggled, and tapped me on the head in reproval. I ignored her, and continued to address my potential offspring.

'If you've got any sense, you'll stay there. It's no fun out here, matey, I can tell you.' A thought struck me. 'Half of us are trying to get back in as it is.'

I put an ear to her tum and listened. Hmmm. Slight sounds, probably breakfast.

'Can you feel it moving?'

Fran laughed and held my head against her. 'Darling, it's half an inch long at the moment.'

'A whole half-inch?' It sounded enormous. I kissed her through the dress, and she pulled my head up and kissed me back.

Now I don't know about you, but whenever this sort of thing starts happening, I get ideas. I got one now.

'Let's make it twins – eh?'

I felt her shake with laughter.

'Shelley, that is not how you make twins.'

'Shut up, pregnant woman.'

I caressed her neck. And discovered, by the merest chance, the zip of her dress. It slid down smoothly. And so it should, it's been slid up and down so many times.

'Shelley . . . ' Fran's voice trembled. 'We can't *again.*'

'What do you mean, again? I've been away an hour.'

The zip slid down further. I could feel the smooth skin of her back. With practised ease, and never separating for a second, we slid over and up the bed, until we were in a position that can only be described as compromising. The zip slid even further, until it reached its terminal point. Fran remembered that fellers have zips too. Simply and swiftly she unzipped a banana.

It was all familiar, yet all as fresh and exciting as the first time. It was about to happen all over again. I was ready. Fran was ready.

And Mrs H. was ready too. There was a loud bang on the door, and then she was in the room, and talking.

'I've got bad news for you, they've got you a job!'

Then she saw us.

'Oh my Gawd!'

I couldn't have put it better myself.

Fran was, of course, her usual splendidly efficient self. She slid smoothly over me, and off the bed, one hand behind her back swiftly returning her zip to its pre-passion position. She shook her hair into place, and smiled at Mrs H. to show there was no harm done.

'Why didn't you tell me you was at it?' complained Mrs Hawkins, adding 'again' as a wistful afterthought.

I'm not quite as quick at getting back to normal as my lovely Fran. Us chaps have problems in this respect. I mean . . . well, remember our first evening in the flat? How I had to stay lying down on the bed, because if I'd got up, I'd have fallen over myself? Well, if I'd got up at this particular moment I'd have pole-vaulted through the window. Bragging again? Yes, bragging again.

Meanwhile I still had a problem. I turned my back to the room, squirmed a bit, and readjusted. Then I carefully re-zipped. *Very* carefully. One can do oneself a nasty.

Mrs Hawkins regarded my contortions with little sympathy or interest.

'That,' she said, still wistful, 'was a new bed when you moved in. My Gawd!'

I grinned at her, and hoped I wouldn't have to get up. I was still extremely indecent, in profile at least. My hopes were not fulfilled.

'You're wanted on the phone,' Mrs H. told me. 'The employment. Come on.'

I shuffled myself across to the edge of the bed, and hunched there. I couldn't get a stupid grin off my face.

'Just a minute, Mrs H.,' I managed.

'Wassamarrer?'

'My emu's playing me up.'

'What?' She clearly thought I was crackers, and I can't blame her.

'Nothing.' I sighed. Fran, curse her, giggled.

Somehow I got myself out of the room. To say I walked would be inaccurate. I 'crabbed', in a kind of Quasimodo crouch, across the carpet and out of the door. Mrs Hawkins watched me go with a cold eye.

And now here's a funny thing. I was able to maintain the

crouch until I got outside the door, and was hidden from view. Then I could stand up. I did so – and I found that the need to disguise my outline had now magically disappeared.

Funny thing, the male body. Too bloody funny.

I knew a virgin once, who could never get laid because as soon as some feller took his trousers off, she started laughing. Oh well . . .

The phone call was brief and to the point. It was Forsyth, and his ability to be provoking was weakened by the wire. I listened, said 'Uh-huh' and 'Okay' a couple of times, and hung up. Then it was back to tell Fran the good news.

Mrs H. was still there, and well into her first cup of tea. She looked intrigued and excited. Fran was flushed. It didn't take a mastermind to deduce that Fran had told her about our expected happy event. I didn't mind. Perhaps the news would somehow provide an excuse not to pay the rent.

Fran looked up, 'Well, what is it?'

'Um, well . . . ' I was hesitant. And you'll soon see why. 'It's only a temporary job. Sort of fill-in for a few weeks. In the pub over the road.'

'The Ship?'

'It's called The Victory now,' and I flinched. The place had predictably been a disaster. In which I was now to become a casualty. 'They want me to run one of the bars.'

Fran smiled at me. 'Well, that's all right.'

I looked soberly back. 'Dressed as Nelson.'

'Pardon?' said Fran, and I don't blame her. Dressed as Nelson, pressing taps for pints of fizzy beer . . . oh my God!

'Still, there's one thing,' I told her.

'What?'

'They say I don't have to have the arm off.'

SEVEN

I WAS awake.

I had been asleep. *Very* asleep. Hundreds of fathoms down in the deepest darkest blackness, somewhere where no absurd sexual fantasy, or episode from school life, or weird association with a member of the Royal Family, or whatever else it is people dream about, could interrupt my beautiful never-ending velvet-lined unconsciousness.

Then I was awake.

I was aware of one thing – that I had had a lot to drink the previous night. There was a certain dryness of the mouth, a certain ache at the back of the neck, a certain remoteness of the limbs. All very familiar. I was hung very far over.

However, as those of us who have graduated from carelessly drinking too much on a Saturday night, and instead now drink too much on a Saturday night on purpose know, a hangover is not the end of the world. Not if dealt with properly, that is. Amateurs get very het-up about hangovers. They have showers, or they drink nauseating hangover cures, or they go for brisk walks, and as a result they feel awful until four in the afternoon. But us professionals know that the answer, the only answer, is sleep, stillness, and rest. So, as an awareness of the previous night's excesses filtered through to my just-dormant brain, I remained just as still as I could, turning just ever-so-slightly to enjoy a long warm lovely cuddle with my long warm lovely Fran. The pillow was soft beneath my head. Hours of nothingness stretched ahead. I didn't have to get up. I didn't have to do anything. I didn't even have to go to work. Ahhhhhhhhh . . .

I didn't have to go to work because last night had been exactly that – my last night. I was shaking the dust of The Ship – or rather, The Victory – from my heels. My employment, as Nelson in The Fo'c'sle bar, had terminated with one big jamboree night commemorating, on entirely the wrong date, the Battle of Trafalgar. The whole affair had been a stunt by the fizzy beer makers – I won't insult an ancient profession by describing them as 'brewers' – and, under the influence of many generous shipmates, Nelson himself had soon been all at sea, not to mention three sheets to the wind.

But, as I lay there that morning, I resolved not to pick over the remains of the previous night. Not yet. Much was still shrouded in alcoholic fog. Perhaps later I would go hot and cold as I recalled some of the things I must have done. But for now, forget it. Forget it. Forget . . .

. . . was there really a moment when I lifted a yard of ale to my right eye, announced 'I see no ships', and poured the rest of the beer in the till? No . . . forget it. Forget it.

The body by my side stirred sleepily. I adjusted myself to it in the old familiar way. My knees into the back of her knees. My middle bit fitting around her bottom. My arm tucked around her slim waist. My face up against her smooth shoulder-blade. Warmth. Comfort. Cosiness. Security. All those things and . . .

. . . something was wrong.

I couldn't put my finger on it, even though my fingers were so close to it all. Something was definitely different. The back of her knees felt . . . awkward . . . her bottom wasn't quite . . . cushiony . . . that rib didn't really feel quite right . . .

Sorry about all the dots in this bit. But that's how I felt at the time – as if bits of life were suddenly slipping away from me, and leaving nothing in their place.

'Mmmmmmmmm . . . ' It was her. Slowly she made those first stretching movements of leg and elbow which meant she was about to roll over on to her back.

Slowly I disentangled myself and began to turn likewise.

'Errrrmmm . . .' I said.

I looked at her. As I looked, she spoke, 'Morning.'

Like a chicken that has had its head chopped off – or so they tell me, I've never actually seen how a chicken behaves when someone decapitates the poor thing – I continued to function almost normally.

'Already?' I asked.

' 'Fraid so.'

It wasn't Fran.

Great God Almighty, no, it wasn't Fran. It wasn't Dracula's daughter, either. It was blonde and fluffy, and its lipstick was smeared, but basically it was quite presentable for first thing in the morning, but it was not Fran.

Where was Fran? Why was this strange woman in bed with me? Fran!

I looked over my other shoulder. For one wild moment I wondered if we'd finally got around to a bit of 'trolleyism'. But no. There was just the side of the bed, and a wickerwork bedside table.

Wickerwork?

My bedside table is plain white builders' deal.

Wickerwork?

My God, I wasn't even home.

I was somewhere else.

Jesus Christ, where?

I stared up at the ceiling. I was most certainly somewhere else. The pattern of cracks in the ceiling plaster was not my pattern of cracks. In my pattern of cracks I could decipher a foaming pint of beer, a couple at it, and a cat. In this pattern of cracks I could read nothing. Except, perhaps, disaster.

She wasn't Fran. I wasn't home.

So who was she, and where was I?

I looked back at the bedside table. On it stood a lamp with a polished wood base. Against the lamp rested a postcard. I snaked a hand out from the blankets, took the postcard, and shot a quick glance at the name to which it was addressed. It said Diana Appleby.

So I was in bed, naked, with Diana Appleby.

Fine. That left just one question.

Who was Diana Appleby?

'Diana,' I said tentatively. Nothing happened. Admittedly my voice was a bit foggy. I cleared my throat, and said it again, louder. 'Diana?'

She looked over at me: 'Who's Diana?'

'Err . . . ' That was what *I* wanted to know.

She saw the postcard in my hand, and clicked.

'My name's Angie.'

It was hardly a time for introductions, I felt. 'Angie, that's right, yes I know, I meant Angie . . . ' I flailed. 'Yes, Angie, I just . . . '

'The postcard,' she said patiently, 'was a present from Laurence.' Then, with just a hint of sarcasm – 'You may have noticed that very few people use penny blacks these days.'

I looked at the card again. It was nearly a hundred years old.

'Ah, yes, yes . . . '

A present from Laurence? Who was Laurence? Wait a minute . . . Laurence! Of course. Good old Laurence, my mate who was a big noise in advertising, and who thought I was a great guy, and who was going to get me a highly paid job because . . .

Laurence! What had I done? What had I done?

Perhaps it *was* time for introductions. 'I'm James Shelley, How d'you do. No, I remembered your name, I just forgot for a moment . . . '

She didn't believe me.

'It's a very pretty card.'

She wasn't buying that, either.

I had to ask: 'Did we . . . ?'

'No.'

Marvellous. Nothing vague. Nothing misleading. A simple abrupt negative. No, we had not got at it. I had been good – or more likely, I had been no good at all. I had not been unfaithful. Waves of relief spread over me like an eiderdown.

'Thank God for that,' I breathed.

Not very tactful. 'Charmed,' said Angie.

'Oh no, I didn't mean . . . ' I began, feeling terrible in more ways than one now.

She shook her head. 'Don't bother.'

But I wanted to bother. 'I mean, I'm sure you're very . . .

well, very . . . *very* . . . ' and from what I could see, she was.

She smiled. 'Well, you seemed quite keen on the idea last night.'

Did I? Oh yes – so I did. The corridor at the back of the pub. I'd just come out of the bottle store. She'd just come out of the Ladies'. Sorry, The Lady Hamilton's. Pretending to dance, then not bothering to pretend anything. Kiss cuddle grope. Oh my God . . .

'Yes, I remember. I'm sorry.'

' 'S alright,' she said. 'I just feel a bit . . .'

'Yes.'

'You know. When nothing happens.'

Quite frankly, she sounded a little pathetic. And I couldn't blame her. Presumably I had approached, she had responded, I had definitely requested, she had acceeded, and then I had . . . done nothing.

And nothing can be more guaranteed to destroy a girl's self-respect than . . . nothing. I decided to try and repair the damage I had caused.

'Oh, it's the height of bad manners,' I said hastily. 'I do apologise. You see, I wouldn't have, err . . . you know, in the first place, if I hadn't been a bit legless.'

I gave her a bright smile, an honest smile. But it began to crack around the edges as I realised just what I'd said.

She realised too. 'I've had a few things said to me,' she remarked coolly, 'but no man has actually ever said he'd have to get drunk to come to bed with me.'

I sank my head back on the pillow. I wished that it was a busy railway line.

'I've got a bad attack of foot and mouth this morning.'

For no particular reason I thought of Fran, and my heart fell over its feet. I could hear birds and traffic. That meant she'd be up by now. Far far too late to try and sneak home.

Yes, Fran would be up by now. She'd be in her long thin red flowing housecoat, that I bought for her last Christmas after selling my Beatles albums. She'd have boiled the kettle. She'd have gone downstairs and collected the post – there was lots these days because I kept applying for jobs, and people kept writing back to say no. She'd have pulled the bed back, tidied the sink, chucked some crumbs out for the pigeons. And now she'd be sitting at the table, drinking her tea, and wondering whether to use my skull as an ashtray or a doorstop. I could almost hear her asking 'Where are you, Shelley?' Answer: I'm lying in Angie's bed, saying tactless things to her.

'It's all right.' Angie gave me a smile. 'I don't suppose you even remember much about last night.'

She climbed out of bed, naked, and slowly struggled into a shortish blue flannel dressing gown. She looked very good indeed, and I wanted to reassure her.

'I remember *everything* about last night,' I claimed. 'In seventy millimetre and Eastmancolour.'

She laughed. She was a nice girl, Angie. I remembered that much. A nice girl for my mate Laurence. Laurence . . . oh dear. How could I have even . . . ?

'I'm really sorry,' I said sincerely. 'I just don't go in for this extra-curricular stuff.'

'What?'

'I mean, I never sleep with anyone except Fran. I'm completely faithful.'

She looked at me, half-believing it. 'Are you really?'

'Totally.' I crossed my heart. 'I try to keep it from her, but that's the way it is.'

She didn't laugh. Instead she said seriously: 'That's really nice.'

I shook my head. 'No, it's just guilt.'

'Ah, you're into guilt, are you?'

'Black belt and bar,' I boasted. 'It was inculcated at an early age. By experts.' This was becoming familiar territory for me at last.

'Who were they?' she asked.

'The usual crowd. In my case, a Miss Ellis was prominent among them.'

'Who was Miss Ellis?'

'A teacher of standard one.' And a teacher of about standard one standard, I thought to myself. 'She suffered from terminal stupidity, and an overriding belief – then very prevalent – that we weren't here to enjoy ourselves.'

Incidentally, that's a view that's still prevalent in some quarters today. The major breweries, for instance. However . . .

'What did she teach?'

'The allocation of blame was her speciality. Everything that happened, whatever it was, was somebody's *fault*. Usually mine. I mean, I always had an uneasy feeling the Suez crisis was down to me. I was only five, but something I'd left undone, a tap running, a cupboard open, had sent Nasser into an acquisitive rage, and impaired Eden's reason.'

All true, this. Perhaps I'm lucky Miss Ellis didn't also burden me with the guilt for the Hungarian Uprising. But little Trevor West got the blame for that. He'd forgotten to fill her inkwell.

'So she filled you up with guilt?' Angie found it funny.

'Oh, they put it in the Farex. Mind you, I registered a protest.'

She sat down beside me on the bed. 'What did you do?'

I looked to both sides, then leaned forward and whispered, 'I got into phantom leaking.'

'What???'

'I'd do it anywhere except the loo. All over the building. I mean, most kids are into urinating, but I was a champ. Up with the short trouser-leg, and out with a succinct comment on the educational system.'

Between giggles, Angie said, 'Didn't they catch you?'

I waved a superior hand. 'I told them Jeremy Hargreaves did it. Jeremy was more absent-minded about his functions than me, and confronted with a puddle he'd always accept ownership with a nonchalance I envied. He was much taken advantage of, not just by me,' I remembered. 'After a while he became the star of the local kidney unit. Student urinologists travelled miles to inspect his genito-urinary apparatus.'

Angie tried to look sorry. 'Poor kid.'

'Not at all,' I pointed out. 'He developed a taste for it. He's a pornographic film star now.'

Angie had a laugh like a peal of bells, and she now gave the ropes a long and vigorous pull.

'What were you protesting at?' she asked.

Time for my real hobby-horse. 'The waste of my childhood,' I said, as if it were obvious. 'Not the best years of your life, but unique. And squandered and made miserable by . . . *teachers*!'

'You weren't that articulate then.'

'Oh yes.' And I was, too. I was a bright kiddie. 'I was seven when I tumbled the truth. Everyone cracks on, it's education. In fact, of course, what happens is, there's a large number of social misfits who would otherwise be a burden on the health and social services. Solution: call them teachers and give them a few million kids to play with. What the hell, they're only kids, we want them out of the way anyway. Two birds with one stone.'

'It's a good speech, that, and in the right company it goes down very well. People have been known to applaud when I finish. Sometimes I take the hat round.

But not today. Angie had become still and silent. I raised an eyebrow at her, wondering what on earth had gone wrong now.

'You don't like teachers much, do you?' she asked.

I tried a joke. 'Oh, there are worse people than teachers – I've never met any, but . . . '

And then I realised. Oh dear. Oh dear oh dear oh dear.

I looked Angie in the eyes. 'You're a teacher, aren't you?'

'Yes.'

Jesus . . .

'Not an awful lot of point in apologising, really,' I suggested.

'No.'

'I mean,' I said, cursing myself, 'I didn't leave too many escape routes.'

'No.'

'Well.' I sank back once again on the pillows and closed my eyes for a second. 'What an absolutely smashing start I've made to the day. What with one thing and another.'

She smiled forgiveness. 'Don't worry about me. I'm not offended.'

'Very good of you.' Then, with care because I didn't want to put my foot in it yet again, 'I must say you're not typical of your profession.'

She gave me a shrewd look. 'You don't think you might be using a rather small sample on which to base your findings?'

' 'Course I am.' I was happy to be generous. 'Probably got it all wrong.'

'Oh, don't take it back, I enjoyed it.'

'Ah.' Not much else I could find to say.

'I mean,' she added, 'I'd rather you didn't wet the bed . . .'

I managed a feeble laugh.

' . . . and don't worry about the other thing.' She meant my non-existent sexual performance. 'Serves me right. I was only using you.'

'Eh?' What was this? Shelley the sex object again?

Angie explained. 'I had a row with Laurence before he left last night.'

'Ah.'

'I was just getting back at him.'

'Good Lord.' Quite a girl, this Angie.

She looked anxious. 'You haven't forgotten you're seeing him today about the job, have you?'

'No.' No, I had not forgotten that today I would see the chap with who's girl I'd just spent the night, and that he would be incredibly decent to me, and I would feel like a worthless rat.

Angie said with a hint of a smile, 'Perhaps we'd best not tell him about last night.'

I grinned back. 'I hadn't planned on sending a telegram. Where'd Laurence go last night?'

'Glasgow.'

'Drive?'

'Sleeper.'

'But I'm seeing him this afternoon.'

'He's flying back.' She said it so casually, too, but I was impressed.

'Blimey, he must be important.'

'Yes.' She looked proud. 'He is quite. He was very pleased about that stunt in the pub, you know.' She meant Nelson's Last Night. 'It was a great success.'

'Good, I'm glad.' Me, I couldn't remember a thing.

She put her head on one side. 'Would you like to work with him?'

'Um, yeah.' As much as I'd like to work with anyone, or at all for that matter. 'Yes, I think I would.'

'He's very keen to have you.'

So were you last night, I thought. But it was an unworthy sentiment, and I wasn't stupid enough to put it into words. Instead, I said, 'Well, that's very nice.'

But the chatting had to stop. Time was a-wasting. By now Fran would have contacted Interpol. I had to get going.

I sat up. My head banged like a rickety turnstile, and a million little black specks, which had been resting on the sea-bed of my eye-balls, now swam up into view.

'Something wrong?' Angie asked.

'Nothing an aspirin and a bit of brain surgery won't put right.'

I climbed gingerly out of the bed. There by the table was my old duffel bag. I opened it. It was empty. Oh no . . .

'I've left my clothes in the pub!'

Angie pointed to the end of the bed. 'The Nelson gear's there.'

It was, too. A pile of gold braid and white knee breeches.

'I can't go home dressed as Lord Nelson!'

'You came here like it.' There was a suspicion of a giggle. Angie was enjoying this.

'I was drunk and it was dark,' I pointed out. 'What we have now is a daylight situation. What am I going to wear?'

'Well . . . ' Angie suddenly brightened. Ah, I'd misjudged her. Bless her, she had an idea. 'Well,' she said, 'I've got a nice Laura Ashley you can borrow.'

She laughed a lot at her own joke. I sat and took it. I know what it's like to get your own back.

Then she did set to and try to help. From a drawer she took a biggish pair of her old jeans – pre-diet, she explained – which came halfway up my shins and just met around the waist with the aid of a giant safety-pin. A t-shirt took care of my top. Over that went a huge mackintosh, which, she claimed, had been hanging in the hall when she originally took over the flat. Finally, on the feet went the Admiral Nelson's very own gilt slippers.

I looked at myself in the mirror. I looked extraordinary.

'You look fine,' Angie told me.

Then she kissed me on the cheek, and slipped me through her front door and out into the great wide unfriendly world.

EIGHT

I DIDN'T want to go home yet. So I went to the newsagent.

'*Guardian*, *Time Out*, and *Advertiser*, please.' A tough-looking lady with blonde streaks gathered them up for me.

By the counter was one of those tall revolving magazine stands. The thing was overloaded with pulchritude, and it was shaking slightly. Could it be, I wondered, the vibrations of the many naked bodies contained within the magazine covers? A whimsical thought for that time of a morning, and, sadly, not true. On the other side of the stand, and now revolving into view with it, were a couple of excited schoolboys, exclaiming in childish wonder at the size of the cover girl's breasts, and the manner in which they defied the laws of gravity. Show that one to the physics master . . .

'Fifty-seven, Sir.' The woman handed me my papers. Then – 'Here, you lot, get away from them. You're not old enough for that yet.'

'They must be,' I pointed out with logic, 'if they are interested.'

'Look here . . . ' She indicated a notice on a magazine cover. It was one of those warnings, as when the BBC announcer talks about 'scenes of an explicit sexual nature' and thus keeps you gripped to the screen for what follows.

'It says "Not for sale to minors",' she said. 'That's all I know.'

I extracted one of the volumes from the rack. 'But she's a

minor – look!' I showed her the girl on the cover. 'She's a schoolgirl.'

She was, too. At least, she wore the uniform and the straw hat, and she was doing something quite remarkable with a hockey stick.

'She's no schoolgirl,' said Madam dismissively.

I flicked through the pages. 'She must be! Look, she's being spanked here.'

Thick navy-blue knickers. Memories of Beryl Wilson.

'All I know is, I'm not allowed to sell these to kids.'

I nodded to the young lads, who were taking advantage of our chat to have further shufties at the goodies.

'Next time they try to beat you at school,' I told them, 'tell them you're not old enough. Go on – be your age and buy a nice war comic.'

They moved off, and I turned back to my salesperson.

'Hey, hang on – can they buy newspapers?'

'Newspapers don't have what them magazines have got?'

I pointed wordlessly at *The Sun.*

'Oh, I know what you mean,' she acknowledged. 'But there's worse in them mags.'

'Really?' Goody gumdrops. I dug deep into the stacks, and came up with something called *Sex Adventures.* The adventures were, one could see at a glance, hardly those of Biggles or Bulldog Drummond.

I flicked through it. 'Good God – they never used to do *that* in Health and Efficiency.'

'*That*' was a photographic sequence of quite devastating incongruity. I mean, in my day, semi-naked ladies romped rather fuzzily through bush and heathland. In this lot, a totally naked gent was consorting with a naked-but-for-regulation-cap conductress on her London Transport vehicle, and they were doing everything except exchange tickets.

I indicated one particular picture, in which a ticket machine was being put to a use for which it was most definitely not designed.

'Now you see,' I told my companion in literature, 'that would never have occurred to me.'

'It's disgusting,' she replied with a sniff.

'Quite right.' I put the magazine down. 'Instant inferiority complex.'

But actually it wasn't. Certain laws about depicting the male genitalia seemed to apply. As a result – and quite appropriately when one considers that the location was a London bus – there was no standing on the upper deck.

I thanked her, picked up my papers, and took a last quick look at the mating display. One cover girl in particular caught my eye. Amazing. She made even my dear café waitress look flat-chested.

'Does this place come under the Milk Marketing Board?' I enquired.

I didn't want to go home yet. So I went to the pub.

'Lo, Shelley,' said Maggie with a smile. 'Pint?'

'No, no.' Any hemlock? I wondered. 'No – soda water.'

'I'm not surprised,' Maggie said with the self-righteousness of the sober. 'After last night. What time did you get back?'

'I've not been back.'

'What? You been out all night?'

'Yeah.'

'Where've you been?'

'Angie's.'

Question and answer. A rehearsal for meeting Fran.

'Oh, Shelley – you didn't?'

'No, I didn't.'

'Well, what's Fran going to say?'

Pass.

'I will have a pint,' I told her. 'Pour it gently.'

She picked up a pint-pot. 'Honestly, you two are getting like an old married couple.'

'About to become an old divorced couple.'

'No.' She shook her head with eighteen-year-old assurance. 'It'll blow over.'

'Yeah. Like Hurricane Flora.' Or Hurricane Frances.

Maggie stuck the glass under the keg spout. She pressed the plastic lever. A squirt, a hiss, a belch – and then finally a dribble of plastic beer.

'God – that stuff's a miracle of modern technology.'

'Yes,' Maggie agreed. 'It is nice.'

'It looks *exactly* like a pint of beer,' I elaborated.

'What?'

'And tastes like tea and liver-salts. Still, I suppose the Inverbraw Grouse Beaters would blow their stack over it.'

Maggie carefully set the brimming pint of sparkling yellow brine down on a dripmat in front of me.

'You sorry it's over, Shelley?'

'Playing Nelson here?'

'Yeah.'

'I quite enjoyed it, actually.' And that was true. 'It wasn't a bad stunt. I'm glad I quit before the death scene though . . . '

'What are you going to do?'

Good question, that. I had a very difficult day in front of me. 'I think,' I said, more to myself than Maggie, 'I'll go to the interview *before* I see Fran.'

'No, I mean, for a living.'

'Well, I think I'm going to get the job,' I pointed out. 'So then I'll have good news.'

'What job?'

'The one I'm being interviewed for.'

Maggie took a long critical look at me. The borrowed gear was no one's idea of an 'interview suit'.

'Clothes are a problem,' I agreed. I sipped the beer. Chemical additives raced each other down towards my shrinking stomach. 'It's amazing,' I observed. 'You can get this stuff off prescription.'

I didn't want to go home yet. But I had to.

I paused at our front door. My retrieved clothes were in my duffel bag. My heart was in my mouth. I found my key, and slipped inside.

Mrs H. was in the entrance hall. She had a letter for me in her hand, and was holding it up against the light.

'Good morning, Mrs H.'

She looked guilty, and put the letter behind her back.

I seized my chance. 'Can I use your loo?'

But she recovered too quickly. 'Well, I'll say one thing for you – you've got guts.'

Why? Because I was prepared to use her loo? No. Quite clearly, because I was prepared to come home at all. Not a good sign.

I held out my hand for my letter, and she gave it to me. 'Thank you, Mrs H.'

'If I was you,' she advised, 'I wouldn't 'ave dared to come back.'

'I need your help, Mrs H.'

She looked pleased. 'She's up there with a meat cleaver. I said I'd 'old you down.'

'You are a sadist, Mrs H. Appealing in its way, I confess, but inappropriate just now. Please,' – I made it a plea – 'can I use your loo?'

'Why d'you wanna use my loo?'

'I want to change. And I don't want to go upstairs, you see, because I don't want Fran to see me yet. That's where I need your help.'

I twisted my face into an eloquent silent appeal. Us Shelleys are a proud breed, but when necessary, we grovel.

'You little worm!'

'Good enough as a character reference, Mrs H.,' I acknowledged. 'Though as a zoological observation I'm bound to say it lacks sophistication. Please, will you help me? For old times sake?'

She rubbed it in. 'I wouldn't 'elp you to an ant's egg if you was starving to death.'

'You're a brick, Mrs H.' I played my trump card. 'If you'll help me, I'll pay the rent.'

'What?' Stunned disbelief. 'All of it?'

Actually, I meant one week. But there was no way out. 'Yes.'

'The 'ole five weeks and the one seventy you nicked from the meter?'

'Full and final settlement.'

'Done!'

And out came a demanding hand.

I'd been paid off the the night before. Plus a bonus. So there was enough. It hurt, though. My God it hurt.

She pocketed the cash, then pointed. 'It's out the back. You 'ave to pull the chain twice.'

I ran for it.

Once inside the Hawkins loo, and gasping from the effects of about seven lavender air fresheners, I stripped off my lunatic clothes and climbed back with comfort into my usuals. I felt better. I felt like Shelley again.

I pattered back through to the front hall again, and checked my hair in the mirror, and smiled sardonically at Mrs H., and . . .

. . . and Fran was at the top of the stairs. Undoubtedly summoned by the traitorous Mrs H.

'Ah,' I managed.

'Lo,' said Fran. All the warmth of an ice-cube.

Mrs H. giggled. 'I dropped you in it, mate,' she crowed.

Fran turned and went back into our flat.

'Mrs H.,' I told the old boot, 'I've always seen myself as pretty immoral. Next to you, I'm Moses the Lawgiver.'

'Well,' she said, with surprising spirit, 'it's time to go up Mount Sinai. And if she's got two tablets of stone, God 'elp you.'

She mimed banging two bricks together. I could almost feel the impact. Slowly, heavily, I walked up the steps of the pillory.

Fran was making our bed with furious energy. I stood behind her, with the clasped hands of the penitent. I could think of nothing original to say, so I settled for something unoriginal but true.

'Look, I'm sorry about last night.'

'That's all right.' It wasn't. 'I didn't expect you back after Trafalgar anyway. Well done, by the way.'

'I got drunk.'

'Shelley, you know you can't hold drink.'

At one stage, I remembered, I'd been holding two drinks in each hand.

'Everyone kept buying me drinks,' I said plaintively. 'Well done at Trafalgar, they'd say. Have one on me, Admiral.'

'Where did you sleep?'

An unfair question, so I ignored it.

'Sorry about the arm, mate, they'd say,' I went on.

'Shelley!' No way out again.

'It's not what it sounds,' I told her.

'What's not?'

'I slept with a girl called Diana.' There, I'd said it. No, wait a sec . . . '*Angie.* Her name was Angie.'

'I see.' A frozen ice-cube. Extra-cold.

'Look . . . '

'Will you give me a hand with this bloody bed?'

'Sorry . . . ' I dumped my magazines and papers on the table, started pulling blankets about, felt useless.

'I mean,' Fran said after a pause for stoking up, 'I know you weren't responsible for messing it up in any way.'

I took a deep breath. 'I occupied her bed all night, but intimacy did not take place.'

'What?'

'We didn't . . . '

'Oh come on!' Total disbelief.

'We didn't, really. Scout's honour,' I vowed.

'Why not? You turned pouffey?'

'Fran!' After all, she should know.

'You just fancied a bit on the side, Shelley,' she went on wearily. 'Like everyone else. Don't be so grand.'

'I didn't. I did not fancy it. It was a mistake. A drunken aberration. I don't want anyone else.' I looked her straight in the eyes, so she could see I meant it.

She looked back, and she saw. 'Don't you?'

'Well . . . ' I was honest. 'Yeah, sometimes, but I'd feel too guilty to do anything about it.'

She shook her head. 'I wish you'd lie to me sometimes. Like any normal man.'

'I don't want to lie to you.'

More head shaking. 'I really can't cope with the George Washington bit.'

'All George Washington did,' I said with some energy, 'was chop down a bloody tree. You tell me what he said when he slept with his best friend's wife, and I'll be impressed.'

'He didn't sleep with his best friend's wife, that's the whole point.'

'Sarah Fairfax in 1755. And he lied like any normal man . . .' This was getting silly. I dragged myself back to the point. 'Look, I'm really sorry about last night.'

I waited. She said nothing.

'You know – sorry,' I tried again. 'That's when you say "Forget it," and we have close physical contact, and the bond between us is further strengthened.'

At last it came – the slightest of smiles, the littlest dropping of the arms in defeat. I took her in mine. I kissed her, she kissed me back. I started fumbling for the good old zipper.

'Stop it, Shelley.'

'Come on,' I urged. 'I haven't had it all night.'

'Sez you.' Still just a trace of doubt, which I had to remove.

'I have not.'

Another kiss. And, well, I couldn't resist it.

'Not a good one, anyway.'

'You bastard!' And . . .

Woooooomph!

She . . . hit me! In the B . . . in the groin. Clenched fist. Hard as she could. Jesus . . .

The world went pink. And buzzed.

When I could speak, I tried not to overreact.

'You slut! You cow! You vicious bitch! Oh . . . Typical bloody woman, always resort to violence. And you always hit me there.'

'Where else?'

'Just 'cos you . . . ouch! . . . wish you had one.'

'Don't give me that sub-Freudian rubbish.' She was very much in control now.

Gradually, I straightened up from the foetal crouch. 'That bloody hurt, you know.'

'Yeah? Well, you hurt me.'

Logic.

'I know. I'm sorry.'

'Well,' and this was the true Fran speaking now, 'act bloody responsibly in future.'

'Look, nothing h . . .' I began another denial but she wasn't interested.

'I *know* nothing happened. I believe you. You're too weedy to do it properly. That's not the point.'

Another bulls-eye, I admitted. 'No, it won't happen again.'

'I should bloody hope not.'

Two or three deep breaths, then I asked: 'Is it over now?'

'I suppose so.' Then, in an entirely different voice, she asked. 'Are you really faithful to me, Shelley?'

'Well . . . ' I prevaricated.

'What?!?'

I confessed: 'I'm having an affair with Mrs H., actually.'

Fran spluttered. 'No you're not. She thinks you're a dead loss. She told me.'

'How do you think she found out?' Then I remembered – 'By the way, I paid the rent.'

'What, all of it?'

'Yeah.'

'Blimey!' Sheer amazement.

'Well, I thought it only right.'

'What?' Sheer disbelief, again.

'The lying old bat cheated it out of me.'

I changed the subject by putting my hand on her tum. 'How's my child?'

'How do you know it's yours?' She asked archly.

'I remember making it.'

'Do you?'

' 'Course I do. It was the autumn one.'

Laughter, and a kiss. It *was* all over. Thank the Good Lord.

'Laurence phoned,' Fran remembered. 'We're going to a restaurant tonight. Him and someone from the firm. What exactly do they do?'

'Advertising agency.' The one I hoped to work for. 'They sell things, you know – cigars, toilet paper, the Tory Party. Laurence arranged the Nelson stunt in the pub.'

'Aren't you seeing him today?'

'Yeah. After the final interview. It's in the bag, I think.' Fingers crossed behind my back. 'Oh, I must remember to take my work for them.'

I found my briefcase and put it on the table, to check that my literary gems were safely inside.

Fran looked over my shoulder. 'Why do they want to see your poetry?'

'Same as advertising,' I explained. 'Saying the most with the least number of words.'

Fran picked up the papers I'd bought, and from within them slipped the bright glossy copy of *Sex Adventures.* She spotted it at once. One could hardly miss those impactive skin tones.

'Must have picked it up by mistake,' I claimed, feeling guilty.

'There's not a jury in the world would believe that.'

Fran flicked through it, and found a group scene, featuring many strange rubber appliances.

'Oh, that's what those things are for,' Fran mused. 'Who's Diana?'

The pace of the question took me off balance.

'Diana? . . . oh yes! Diana! Diana Appleby.'

'Who is she?'

'Dunno,' I said honestly. 'But a friend of hers was in Margate in 1893.'

NINE

TEACHERS, PARENTS, youth leaders, all those who during my life have known better than me, have always said that the important thing in an interview is to make a good impression.

Wrong again.

The important thing is to make as little impression as possible. Be flat, be plain, be bland. Be two-dimensional. Let the interviewers do the hard work.

The alternatives are, in my case, fatal. If I put on the conventional act as an upcoming, go-getting, quick-thinking, arse-licking young executive, interviewers will suss me out, no bother. If they don't, then inevitably I will start sending myself up, and the whole thing will end in chaos. Alternatively, if I sit there and tell them what I really think and believe . . . then, well . . . they'll know what I really think and believe. End result in both cases – no job.

My interview on this traumatic day was with several rather sleek executives from Laurence's advertising firm. I wanted the job, so I made no 'impression'. Instead I listened to them carefully, while they told me all about myself. I agreed with them when they summarised my career thus far. I learned a lot about what I would like to do in their agency. I hardly said a word. In the end they had a good old set-to about how much money I wanted, argued it back and forth, and settled on a compromise figure. My agreement was a formality.

No actual offer of a job was made. But Laurence, who slipped in for a quick chat with the executives afterwards, was cockahoop. They were very impressed, he said. An offer was definitely on its way, and could he have my work samples once again, because someone else wanted to see them?

'Sure.'

I handed them over.

We were in The Victory again. It was early evening, five thirty, and a long night of dinner with Laurence and his colleague stretched ahead. But a celebration pint was obligatory.

Laurence got the drinks. He's a good lad.

'Well, cheers.'

'Cheers.'

I sipped at my pint of petroleum extract with caution. It fizzed on my tongue, nibbled my enamel, and set off to see what damage it could do to my small intestine. Why do people make such muck? I wondered yet again. Why bother?

'I'm glad you're into beer,' Laurence said, downing half his gin and tonic. 'This'll be your first account.'

'What?'

'This.' He tapped my pint of poison. 'Its sales are declining – I don't know why.'

'I do.' Something to do with the death rate, perhaps.

'Jolly good.' Laurence was pleased. 'That's what I thought, and we've got the account, so I thought you'd be the ideal man.'

He wasn't joking. He was serious.

I took a deep breath. 'You mean, my first job will be to get as many people as possible to drink . . . this?'

'That's it.'

I was near to panic. He didn't know what he was asking. To connive in funnelling this lighter-fuel down the throats of innocent civilians . . . we couldn't hope to get away with it for ever. Soon there'd be the exposures in *The Sunday Times*, the photographs of the twisted bodies of keg drinkers, the public enquiries, the tribunals . . . My God, thalidomide would pale in comparison. And was I now to become one of the Guilty Men?

Laurence downed the other half of his gin, and waved his glass at mine. 'Mind you, I can't understand what you guys see in this stuff. I think it's foul, quite frankly. Looking forward to tonight?'

'Oh yes.' If I survived this pint.

'It's a good restaurant, we should have a nice evening.' He looked critically at my glass again. 'Do you ever brew your own beer?'

'No.' I took a drink and thought about it. 'But a chap called Jeremy Hargreaves and I used to make a lot of this at one time.'

'*Standard*, please.'

'You nicked it, didn't you!'

Blonde streaks in the newsagent's had remembered me.

'Pardon?'

'That special interest book.'

Special interest? It's not that special, is it? I thought we were all of us interested in the subject. Most of us, anyway.

'I took it by mistake,' I told her.

Her reaction mirrored Fran's. 'Don't make me laugh.'

'You ever done jury service?' I asked, remembering what Fran had said exactly. She was probably right, no jury would believe me. I looked in my briefcase for the offending periodical, and it wasn't there.

'Haven't you gorrit?'

'I appear to have lent it to a friend.'

'Eighty-five pee. And you're lucky I haven't called the police.'

I found a crumpled pound note for her. 'If the police saw it, they'd close you down.'

'They would not!'

She was very very confident about it. Too confident. Light dawned . . .

'No, I suppose not. They're probably running the place.'

Out, quickly. And home, James . . .

Mrs Hawkins came right out with it, as one would expect.

I was in the entrance hall at the time, peering into the wall mirror to straighten my tie and ruffle my fringe. Fran was upstairs in the flat, using our only mirror. I took a long critical look at myself. I was wearing my suit – at least, it would have been a suit if the trousers matched the jacket – and I thought I looked pretty good. The smart young advertising executive . . .

' 'Ow much d'you make then?'

I sighed, and told Mrs H. what my new job paid.

'What? Every week?'

'Yes.'

'Dear Gawd in 'eaven!'

I have to admit, it did sound a lot. I'm not going to tell you how much it was. It impressed me and Mrs H. all right, but by the time you read this, England's galloping inflation will have reduced it to a derisory sum. However, for that particular moment in time, it was really quite splendid.

Mrs H. expressed her happiness at my good fortune in her usual generous manner.

'My Willie don't get 'alf that, and 'e's always doing overtime. And you walk straight into that. It's never right in all this world.'

'Couldn't agree more, Mrs H.' I wasn't kidding, either.

'Well, one thing's for sure.' She folded her arms aggressively. 'You can pay your rent on time from now on.'

'In advance, Mrs H.,' I declared with a flourish. '*And* we'll put it up a bit.'

'What?' I could see all her fillings.

'And . . . ' I produced a couple more quid. 'This is for a new lock on the meter. Replace the one I broke.'

She wobbled. I thought for a moment she was going to faint.

'What are you up to?'

'Just giving in to irrational guilt, Mrs H.' I turned back to the mirror. 'Something I've had to learn to live with.'

She still stood there, her mouth still open. I decided to give her a real treat. After all, guilt might make me pay her properly. But it said nothing about pulling her leg.

I winked at her reflection. 'And I do fancy you, you know.'

'Eh?'

'Only Fran seems to think I haven't made that clear.'

'Wharreryouonabout?'

She inched back towards her door. I turned, arms out, seductive smile on.

'I'm just not an outgoing individual – but that doesn't mean I don't lust after the fruits of your body.'

Mrs H. clasped her hands over two of the fruits. 'You dirty sod!'

'Oh, you've found out!' I wrapped my arms around her. She smelled of Dettol.

' 'Ere!' She struggled free. Well, it wasn't that tight an embrace. 'Wharrer you doin'?'

'What do you think I'm doing, Mrs H.? Or can I call you Beryl?' I sounded like Groucho Marx.

'Me name's Edna!'

'I've often wondered. What a lovely name. Edna.'

'Mrs H. to you! 'Ere, what would your Fran say if she . . .'

I raised a hand with assurance. 'Oh, I've cleared it with Fran, Edna.'

'Mrs H.! 'Awkins!' Rising panic. 'Cleared what?'

'I'm sorry I've been such a dead loss.'

'I 'aven't cleared nuffin' with my Willie!'

'Ah, but then we have to face these things in life . . . ' I moved in closer.

'Oh yeah?' Give her credit, she fought back. 'Well, what about if it was my Willie and your Fran? Eh? 'As that been cleared? Eh? Can we face that? Eh?'

I smiled. 'Oh, you know about that. Good.'

'Know about what?' Desperation! 'There's nothing going on between Willie and Fran . . . ' And after a long second thought, 'There couldn't be . . . '

Brrrrrring! Saved by the door bell!

'I'll gerrit!'

Fran appeared at the head of the stairs, dolled up and delicious.

'You've come just in time,' Mrs H. told her. ' 'E's an animal!' She opened the door with a jerk.

Laurence and Angie stood on the step. 'Hello, are you Mrs Shelley?' Angie asked. I could have kissed her.

'What???' She made it plain she wasn't.

'I thought you might be Shelley's mother,' Angie explained.

‘’E hasn’t got a mother, love. ’E came in on a meteor, and they can’t find the antidote.’ One of Mrs H.’s better lines, that one.

‘Hello James,’ said Laurence. And as Fran joined me, he clearly wanted introductions.

‘Ah, Fran, this is Laurence. Laurence – Fran.’

I could feel myself reddening as they said their how-do’s. Angie was waiting, looking expectant. I had to introduce her to Fran. Oh help. I put it off for a moment.

‘And . . . err . . . Mrs Hawkins . . . Laurence.’

More formal greetings. Then everyone waited. And looked at Angie. I nerved myself for it.

But Fran, dear Fran, didn’t wait for me. She got in first. She leaned forward, held out a hand, and said to Angie, ‘Well, you must be Diana!’

And as she did so, she put her left stiletto down very hard on my blue suede.

Dinner was terrific. You could tell by the prices.

I mean, I personally ate about eight quid’s worth of vichysoisse and salmon, and I took it easy. Fran, on the other hand, was probably trying to prove some point about the starving Asiatics, and happily chomped through smoked trout and two or three priceless little roasted birds, putting another eleven quid on the bill and another two inches on her waistline. I found comfort in the thought that this would soon come off again with regular nightly exercise. Laurence and Angie did not stint, either, although I noticed that Laurence kept his slim-line young executive image in mind with asparagus and plain steak, and I had personal knowledge that the extra Angie was taking on board, in the shape of pâté and Boeuf en croûte, would not come amiss around those ever-so-slightly skinny ribs.

However, if we four were giving way to our appetites, we were outdone by our host for the night and his wife. They ate and drank as if there was no tomorrow. And as my doctor would say, eat and drink like that and there may be a tomorrow, but there will be no next year.

Their names were Cyril and Geraldine, which is not their

fault. Cyril was a mid-forties advertising executive, and Geraldine was his bored and waspish wife. Which *is* their fault. I mustn't be too mean. They were good-natured, and generous to a fault. They were just . . . well, not my sort of people. Oh, come on, Shelley – don't be a snob!

And they could drink. Oh boy! By the time the waiters came round with the pudding trolley, we could have gone ten-pin bowling with the wine bottles. By then, in any case, we were into shorts. Cyril was sweating pure alcohol. Geraldine ate an After-Eight with the wrapper on, and didn't notice. It was developing into quite a night.

Cyril raised a glass, drained it, and declared to the entire restaurant, 'That was the worst Scotch I've ever drunk.'

'I'm not surprised.' I kept my voice a little lower. 'It was, in fact, my crème de cacao.'

'Really?' Cyril was unmoved. 'Well, it wasn't up to much as crème de cacao, either.'

Sorry about the poncey drink. I'm a beer man, first and last.

Geraldine focused on her husband with difficulty. 'Cyril,' she announced, also to the entire assembled company, 'you're drunk.'

'Thank God for that! Thought for a while I wasn't going to make it.' He roared with laughter, and drained another glass. This time it was his Scotch. Then he turned expansively to me.

'Well, Shelley, there we are, very glad to have you aboard.'

He'd begun the evening by announcing confirmation of my appointment to the agency, this fact remaining an excuse for all the booze consumption.

'Thank you,' I said. Not for the first time.

'I'm sure you'll do well,' he went on generously. 'Your work was first-class.' Laurence had passed my stuff on to him. Cyril winked. 'By the way, reminds me – there was a magazine in with it.'

Ah! So that's where *Sex Adventures* had got to. It *was* having an adventure.

'Yes,' I admitted, with the feeling I'd been here before. 'I picked it up by mistake.'

'Oh come on!' He chuckled richly.

'You know,' I told Fran, 'I'm very worried about the jury system.'

She remembered, and giggled.

Cyril was still going on about the magazine. 'Full of naked men and women, up to the most extraordinary things.'

'Lucky them.' That was Geraldine.

'Beats the figure section in *Amateur Photographer*,' I agreed.

'One man in it . . . ' Cyril wiped his forehead. 'Well, it was quite extraordinary. I wouldn't have thought it possible, quite frankly.'

Angie, who'd been following all this with interest, now remembered part of my embarrassing chat with her that morning.

'I expect it was Jeremy Hargreaves,' she suggested.

'Who?' Cyril wanted to know.

'He started very young,' I said, hoping he might blow over. But he didn't.

'How do you know about Jeremy?' Fran asked Angie – and then answered her own question. 'Oh yes . . . ' Her eyes gleamed.

'Jeremy who?' Laurence asked in his innocence.

Fran and Angie began to exchange confidences.

'Did you get Miss Ellis and the phantom leaking?'

'Yes,' from Angie.

'The running tap, the open cupboard, and the Suez crisis?'

'That's right.'

'I'm terribly sorry,' bumbled Cyril, 'I think I've lost the thread of this.'

'You're drunk, Cyril,' Geraldine told him, having a bit of tongue trouble with 'Cyril'.

Fran was still at it. 'He covered the ground then,' she told Angie. 'How about Miss Clark and the sex instruction?'

'No . . . ' Angie thought hard. 'No, I think I missed that.'

'I'll stop by sometime,' I put in, with a hard look at Fran. 'Won't take a minute.'

'It was quite good actually.' Angie was anxious to avoid trouble.

'Oh yes, what he says is right enough,' said Fran. 'It's just becoming a bit of a golden oldie.'

'Angie's a teacher, Fran,' I warned. I was anxious to avoid trouble, too.

'I mean, he's a bit bigoted about some things,' Fran said hastily.

Poor old Cyril was several whiskies behind the rest of us, conversationally speaking. 'Sorry, I mean, I was just talking about this sex thing . . .'

'That's all you ever do.' Geraldine seized her chance. '*Talk* about it.'

'You're drunk, Geraldine!'

'I think,' I said loudly, 'it's past the waiter's bedtime, actually.'

'Yes, I suppose we'd better be going.' Cyril looked around for other glasses to empty. 'Well, Shelley, I look forward to starting on the beer with you, eh?'

'What?' He couldn't mean . . . no, of course – the keg account. 'Oh yes.'

'Mind you, not all our products are as good as that.'

'Ah.' Jesus!

'We're breaking you in gently, as it were.'

'Very kind.'

'Yes, I'm afraid we sometimes have to sell the most awful rubbish.'

My God, what else could he mean? Nazi armbands?

'Still, that's the name of the game,' he went on jovially. 'Never mind selling fridges to Eskimos, we've got to sell lousy fridges to Eskimos, Eh?'

And he blew his nose long and loudly on the bill.

In bed later on, warm and weary . . .

'Sorry about last night.'

'Forget it. I quite liked her, actually.'

Mmmmmm. I cuddled her tum. No wonder Fran ate so much. She was eating for two.

'Have you thought about what we're going to call it?'

'Well,' Fran said definitely, 'it won't be Cyril.'

I groaned slightly at the prospect of working with the man, then added, 'Or Geraldine.'

'You could do another job.'

'No point.'
A warning: 'I won't live with a martyr.'
'No, no.' I waited.
'What's wrong?' she asked.
'Well . . .'
'What?'
'Something I want to know.'
'What?' A little exasperated.
I went quiet and serious. 'Will you tell me the truth?'
'Of course.' She didn't like this.
'Promise?'
'Yes! What is it, for Chrissake?'
I held her close, protected my vulnerable parts as best I could, and whispered: 'Are you having an affair with Mr Hawkins?'

TEN

FOUR DAYS shalt thou labour, and do all that thou hast to do. And on the fifth day thou shalt hang about at the cashier's window, waiting for thy pay.

It was difficult to believe that I had at last managed a week in a legitimate job, and was about to collect my first legitimate pay packet. But it was true. The notice said that pay being collected could be picked up any time after ten-thirty on a Friday morning. And there I was, tapping on the window at a time which I could confidently state was 'after ten-thirty'. To be precise, it was ten-thirty and twenty seconds. Can you blame me? I was about to become rich. Rich, I tell you! Rich!

Such an auspicious day had begun quite normally with what I call the Seven O'Clock Chase, in which half-asleep Fran is pursued across the sheets by fully-aroused Shelley. Healthy morning exercise, it is. You see, if the chase is unsuccessful, and I don't catch her, then at least I keep fit. And if I do catch her . . . well, at least I keep fit. Be honest, it's better than jogging.

'Shelley!' She slid away from me. Not an encouraging start.

I moved in again.

'Shelley, stop it!'

'Mmmm.' Meaning 'why not?'

'There's no time. The alarm's about to go off.'

'So am I.'

A muffled giggle. 'Should have thought of that last night.'

'I was too drunk.' Legless, in fact.

'It was an excuse.' More giggles. 'You'd only had a couple of pints.'

'Couple of pints!' Six, to be precise. 'Come on, I was laid out.'

'Well, I know *I* wasn't!'

I regarded that remark as a challenge.

'Gerroff, Shelley!' An elbow in the stomach. 'Go to work. Win some bread.'

I went to work. On her.

'Oooooh!' Pushed off again. 'Listen, you get paid today.'

I stopped. 'Is it Friday?'

'Yes.'

'Thank God!' I rolled back on to my pillow, closed my eyes, stretched. 'Two lie-ins coming up!' I realised I was feeling some of the euphoria that must be general amongst the working population on a Friday. Two whole days off!

'I hate working for a living,' I told Fran as we lay shoulder to shoulder, hip to hip. 'I was happy as a layabout. It was my calling, you know. I could've made a successful career of that.'

'Fool.' Sometimes she is a blunt lady.

'I could've,' I protested. 'I'm wasted working. It's a personal tragedy.'

'Don't talk cock, Shelley.' Sometimes she is an inelegant lady. 'You're loving every minute of it.'

'Eh?' Now she'd gone crackers.

'You are,' Fran insisted. 'Strutting about as the important young executive. You've been a new man since Monday.'

'Well, it's all right, I suppose.'

There was some truth in what Fran said. On Tuesday evening, for instance, I'd found myself practising my signature in order to sign memos with a flourish. Wednesday lunchtime, and I was discussing with Laurence the relative merits of Grouse Scotch whisky and Johnny Walker Scotch whisky. And I don't even drink the stuff. Was I going soft? Was this the end of Shelley, poet, rebel, and philosopher? Was it hell!

'It must be killing you that you like doing what everyone else does,' Fran said dryly.

I grinned. 'I'll live.'

'You get paid a bomb as well, don't you!' She could still hardly believe it. 'We're going to be rich.'

'Yeah, I suppose we are. Fairly rich,' I quibbled. 'By our standards.' And then, 'How's our child?'

Fran looked down at her outline in the bed. There was still hardly the slightest sign.

'It hasn't grown much,' she said, and there was a note of disappointment in her voice. I guessed that, as a proud mother-to-be, she couldn't wait to be walking around in dresses from Marquee and Spencer, ho ho.

Then, with a tinge of worry, she added, 'It's going to be awkward when I'm . . . big, isn't it?'

She meant making love. I put a comforting and non-prurient arm around her. 'Doesn't matter.'

She snuggled closer. 'Doesn't it?'

'No. I shan't fancy you then anyway.'

I was spared a punch in the ribs by the alarm clock, which abruptly shrieked into life. It was seven-thirty. It was getting-up time. Time to leap out of the pit, do twenty push-ups, and head for the shower and the scented soap with a spring in the step and a song on the lips.

I turned it off, rolled over, and shut my eyes.

'There is no hope,' I told Fran, 'for a civilisation that starts its days to that noise.'

'Gerrup!' Not much sympathy there.

'It's true.' I decided to expand by theme. 'Have you ever thought about it? It's the little things that are the giveaways. Never mind the wars – we can rationalise those – it's that noise that your Martian couldn't believe. Everybody violently awoken every morning by that deliberately offensive clatter. Who but a nutcase could've dreamed it up? Nightmared it up. A mechanical automatic nooky-stopper.'

Pretty profound, that, I thought.

Fran said, 'There's nothing worse than profundity before breakfast.'

'I wish Leboyer would look at alarm clocks.'

Fran was pretty unmoved by all this. You know those moments when you, say, are enlarging on the role of nuclear power in Britain during the first half of the twenty-first century, and the lady in your life remarks that blue gingham would be perfect for the kitchen curtains? This was one of them.

'Do you think,' she wondered, 'as you're going to get paid, do you think we could do something tonight? You know, like real people – go to the theatre, or a restaurant, or see a film less than forty years old?'

'Why not?' I yawned, ignoring the sarcasm about 'real people'. 'Let's do all three.'

Oh, bed felt good. Cuddle, cuddle . . .

'Oh come on, Shelley! Mrs H.'ll be up in a minute to give us a knock.'

That was true. Mrs Hawkins had appointed herself my unofficial time clock – which, sadly, I was not allowed to punch.

I put on my best Mrs H. voice. 'You was late leaving again today,' I screeched. 'You'll lose that job.'

And Fran joined me in unison for the refrain, 'I don't know what you do in that bathroom!'

'I'll give her a knock one of these days,' I threatened. I'm at my most vindictive in the mornings. 'What a woman! She should marry your father.'

I shouldn't have said that. I knew it, as soon as my lips stopped waggling. Too late now.

'Oh my God!' Fran half sat up. 'Don't start on again about my father.'

'I'm not starting, I just . . .'

'I can't help my father.'

'I know, only . . .'

'You're always on about him, Shelley!'

'I'm not.'

But I suppose I am. The whole conversation sounded familiar.

'He's not that bad, anyway,' Fran said defensively.

'He's very nice. He makes Ivan the Terrible look like Santa Claus, but he's . . .'

She sat up even straighter and glared at me. 'He's a much more liberal man than you think.'

'Ha!' I exploded. 'He's about as liberal as Genghis Khan.'

There was a brief silence. The cosiness of early-morning-in-bed had gone. Icicles hung from the headboard.

'Shelley,' Fran began, in tones which said she was going to be reasonable and polite, even in the face of such outrageous provocation, 'I do wish you'd make an effort to know him. It's not all on one side, you know. What made you think of him, anyway?'

'I've thought of him every morning since Monday.'

'Why?'

''Cos I know he'd approve of my getting up and working for a living. And I can't bear that.'

Fran wanted to laugh, but she suppressed it with her iron will.

Instead, after a moment, she said, 'You've upset me now.'

'No I haven't.' I pulled her back down. 'Give us a kiss.'

'I mean, I can't help . . . ' She didn't get any further. But I did. A long kiss led to another one. Hands moved into action. Breathing quickened. For a moment it looked as if the Seven O'Clock Chase was going to end in a kill.

Thump, thump, thump!

No, it wasn't two hearts beating as one. Neither was it the bed-head rocking against the wall. It was the fist of Mrs H. on the door.

'Time to gerrup! Wakey, wakey!'

We will draw a discreet veil over exactly what I bellowed back at the old boot. Let us also ignore my general bad-tempered showering, dressing, eating of toast, clattering downstairs, trundling off to work, and so forth. Let us come right up to the moment with which I began. Remember – I was standing outside the cashier's window, waiting for my pay, and tapping my fingers impatiently on the glass.

'Time to gerrup!' I said, avoiding the stridency of Mrs H. 'Wakey, wakey!'

The window slid back. Two brilliant blue eyes, an up-tilted nose, and straw-blonde hair in a schoolgirl fringe. I gave her my name, then watched as she sorted through a drawer-full of wage packets.

Very nice she was. Seventeen. Pure white blouse. Trim dark blue skirt. Virginal, I guessed – and hanging on to it by means of some frantically heavy petting.

Yes, yes, I know it's outrageous to form such judgements about total strangers. But it helps to pass the time.

The little darling proved her worth when she located my little brown darling packet. I took it, and began fumbling with the sealed flap. It felt satisfactorily bulky.

'Your first one, Mr Shelley?' A sweet smile, but lipstick on the teeth. Never mind.

'Yes.'

'Shall we pay it straight into the bank from now on?'

I gave her my serious, worried look. 'I don't think that would be a good idea.'

'Why not?'

'I haven't got a bank account.'

She stared at me blankly. No sense of humour. Oh well . . . I opened my envelope, pulled out the pay slip, looked at it.

Oh, no. Oh no no no no no. No.

'You've given me the wrong pay.'

'Have I?'

'Yes.' I showed her the slip. 'I agreed a slightly higher figure than that.'

She was very nervous now. Perhaps she thought I'd start foaming at the mouth and tearing my shirt off. Wise girl. That's exactly what I felt like doing.

'It does say . . . ' she began carefully, but I interrupted.

'Yes, yes. My name's on it. But it's not right.'

'Just a minute . . . ' She found a huge sheet of paper covered in figures, and she compared it with my pay slip. 'It is right. Look.'

I looked. 'Yes, that's right – but that's not what's in the packet.'

'Yes,' she insisted, 'look!' And she showed me another figure.

'What's that?'

'That's the net pay. After deduction.' Her voice trembled.

'They can't deduct that much!'

'I'm afraid so.' She was near tears now.

'Not without a gun and a getaway car.' I gave her a big grin to ward off the actual weeps, and was rewarded with a rather watery smile.

'Tax, stamp, and graduated pension,' she explained.

'No . . . ' I couldn't believe it. 'The Mafia would leave me more than that. All I've got here is me bus fare home and a fish supper.'

'It is right.'

'You mean, they actually take that much? And keep it? Every week?'

'Yes.'

'And people take it lying down . . . ' My voice reached a rather strained pitch.

'Well . . . ' She shrugged delicate little shoulders. The white blouse slipped a little. A purple love bite sprang into view. Did I say 'virginal'? I forced my mind back to money.

'It's lunacy,' I told her. 'I got this much on the dole.'

'Did you?'

'Well, the difference isn't worth the sacrifice. I gave up a successful career for this. Oh no . . . ' I shook my head. 'This can't be right.'

The girl checked her list again, then looked up with sympathy, like the surgeon breaking the news that it'll have to come out.

'You're on the highest coding,' she said.

Highest coding? What was I, a spy? The fifth man?

'Tax code,' she explained.

'Why?'

'I don't know.' She smiled. She'd thought of a way out. 'Better ask the tax people.'

I sighed. 'Where are they?'

'Walpole Street.'

I nodded. Walked away. I could almost hear her sigh with relief. I went about six steps, turned, came back again. Her face fell. I leaned on the ledge by her window, and looked deeply down into the front of her blouse.

'Do they carry guns?' I asked.

The girl behind the income tax office counter was made of tougher stuff. Or perhaps she was just more accustomed to dealing with nutters. She took me in her stride.

'Yes sir, can I help you?'

'Where's the head robber?' Well, why not?

'I beg your pardon, sir?'

'The chief brigand,' I insisted. 'Where is he?'

She sighed. Heard it all before. 'Do you have a tax query, Sir?'

'No.' I waved my pay slip. 'I've been burgled.'

'Just one moment, Mr . . . ?'

'Shelley. James Shelley.'

She nodded. Ice-cool. Then she turned and glided away. There's something incredibly sexy about such efficient, imperturbable ladies. Nice shape too. Hmm . . .

In the office behind the counter sat some poor bloody pen-pusher of about my age. I decided to strike up a conversation, perhaps even lighten his day. Or mine.

'I've just given money, you know.' Pride, self-satisfaction – just like Hancock in 'The Blood Donor'. Get it?

'Sir?' He didn't.

'Do you give money?'

'What's that?' He didn't have experience in coping with loonies, either.

'Quite easy,' I told him. 'At work. They come round. No pain. Although mine must be a rare type. They took lots of it.'

'I'm awfully sorry . . . '

'Still, cup of sweet tea and a biscuit, I should be all right.'

He opened and shut his mouth. Then, 'Is Miss Gibbs attending . . . ?'

'Quick lay-down,' I finished.

Miss Gibbs returned. Pen-pusher sighed with relief.

'Mr Shelley?' Still cucumber-cool.

'Yes?'

'Would you come this way?'

She tip-tapped her way down a parquet corridor, with me shambling at her elbow. I tried one more . . .

'What do you think of Ronald Biggs?'

'Sir?'

'As a fellow professional, I mean.'

She didn't have time to answer. Or to cuff me around the ear, as I'm sure she longed to do. Instead, we were there. The door said 'Hewitson'. She opened it, and ushered me through.

'Mr Shelley, sir.'

ELEVEN

AND SO once more it was the classic confrontation. Shelley versus authority.

I'd spent years confronting other representatives of the powers that be – parents, social security men, professors, doctors, public house landlords – but I'd never before come knowingly face to face with a taxman. And I have to admit that Mr Hewitson came as a pleasant surprise, in appearance if not in character or behaviour. For instance, he did not, I noticed, have a large dorsal fin protruding from his back. And when he opened his mouth, I was quick to spot that he did not have three layers of overlapping front teeth all pointing backwards. He was late fifties, with the moustache and haircut that speak of wartime RAF, and the tan that speaks of Spanish holidays. All very normal – except for one thing. One of his more prominent incisors had an outline of gold. Yes, gold. *My* gold. My resolve hardened.

Hewitson himself was, I thought, about to receive an unpleasant surprise. Something in his manner told me he was accustomed to complaints. All manner of bewildered and impoverished tax payers must have wandered bleating into this little office. Hewitson's job was blandly to assure them that all was well, that they had no legitimate grievance, and that they should get back out there on the shovel, and earn some more cash for the Inland Revenue. No doubt it was an art in which he was practised and successful, for he exuded an air of relaxed confidence. There was no question, one felt, which Hewitson could not answer. No objection which he could not counter. No denunciation which he could not cause to founder and appear ridiculous. Everything about him said 'I am Super-Authority. I am Invincible!!'

Yes. Well. He'd never met a Shelley, had he!

'Mr Shelley, sir.'

'Thank you, Miss Gibbs.' The door closed behind me.

A fake smile, a gesture to a chair. 'Do sit down, Mr Shelley.'

Oh, no. Oh no no no no. We weren't going to start like that. We were not going to begin this interview the Hewitson way. We were going to begin it the Shelley way. And rule one of the Shelley way is – never sit down when they tell you to.

Instead, I stood across the desk from him, produced my pay slip – which was beginning to look just the slightest bit dog-eared – and slapped it down on his blotter.

Hewitson took it and read it. Then he re-read it. Then he read it again. He seemed to be struggling to decipher it. What did he think it was, a John le Carré novel? And after all, *he* wrote it. Him or his minions. I stood at the desk and looked down at him, my face a mask of irate determination. Have you ever noticed how difficult it is to maintain a mask of irate determination – or even determined irritation – when no one's looking at you?

However, just when the corners of my mouth were beginning to ache, Hewitson decided that he'd read enough for today, thank you, and he pushed the pay slip back across the desk to me.

He looked up, as if waiting for me to say something. I looked back in silence. What was the point in talking? It was all down there in black and white. Daylight robbery.

'Now . . . ' Ah, yes, he was urbane all right, this one. He made the inspector at the D of E sound like Arthur Mullard. 'Now . . . how can I help you?'

I didn't mess about. 'Just give it back right away, and we'll say no more about it.'

'Give what back, Mr Shelley?'

'The booty. The swag.'

Hewitson sat back in his chair, his face displaying a kind of quizzical concern. It was the sort of look that politicians give Robin Day when he's being particularly stroppy.

'I'm afraid I don't understand,' he said.

I leaned across and shoved the pay slip literally under his nose.

'See the top figure?'

'Yes?'

'See the bottom figure?'

'Yes?'

'There is a grievous discrepancy.'

'That's income tax.' A man for the obvious, Hewitson.

'Well, I'm sorry.' I sat down. By now he'd forgotten he told me to. I rested an arm on the desk. 'I'm sorry. I appreciate the honour and all that, but I'm simply not prepared to fund the nation's economy single-handed.'

He took a moment or two to work that one out, and when he did he was annoyed.

'Mr Shelley, I'm a very busy man.' I'm sure he was. With so much of other people's money to collect. However . . .

'That scale of taxation,' I pointed out, 'is preposterous. That's not deduction, it's amputation. It makes the Godfather look like a shop-lifter.'

He sighed, and half rose from his chair. 'Now, Mr Shelley, you've had your joke, can we . . . ?'

'Joke?' I almost shouted. Hewitson sank back in his chair under the impact. 'Joke? If you call that a joke, mate, I'd hate to be around when you get serious. Where do you go for a good night out? The crematorium?'

'Mr Shelley!' He was out of his chair again.

I held both hands in the air. 'Yes, I'm sorry. I'm sorry. No, no, really, please. Sit down, sit down, it's okay. I know, I know. I was a bit . . . I'm sorry.'

Hewitson wavered, then sat down again.

'I apologise for my attitude when I came in,' I told him. 'I was in a state of shock. I'd just had my money removed.'

He twitched a bit at that, and I went on. 'I mean, I had not anticipated quite so large a tax deduction from my salary.'

He relaxed. We were back with words he understood. 'Yes, I think I'd grasped that, Mr Shelley.'

I leaned forward, all serious and solemn. 'In the interest of establishing common ground, will you agree that my contribution to the nation's well-being is on the generous side?'

'Oh, it's the maximum possible.' He smiled. 'You only have the minimum allowance.'

'I'm sorry?'

'You're not married, Mr Shelley?'

'Well, only in the eyes of God, so to speak.'

'Which is . . . ' He hesitated, gave a little chuckle. I knew the signs. Authority was about to make a joke. Hold on to your sides, they may split.

'Which is . . . ha ha . . . very fine as far as it goes, but . . . ha ha . . . *He* doesn't seem to have passed the message on to the coding department of the Inland Revenue.'

That was the joke. It sat on the desk between us, shrivelling. I waited. The longer I waited, the more it shrivelled. Jokes are like that.

Finally I said, 'Very good.'

'Oh well . . . ' A deprecatory wave of his hand.

'No, no,' I insisted. 'Nice one. Very funny.'

'You're very kind.' Another wave.

'Not at all.' And then I added, 'Sorry about the crematorium.'

'Oh, Good Lord . . . ' A forest of waving hands now, which he suddenly decided looked silly, and dropped into his lap.

'No, no, that was very rude,' I told him, penitently. 'Can't imagine what made me say it. I mean . . . '

'Think nothing of it,' Hewitson broke in. 'After all . . . ' he was trying for another one, 'you were in post-operative shock.'

'Yes.' I gave him a broad smile. Held it just a little too long. He began to look uneasy again.

'So you're not married,' he went on. 'Do you have any children?'

'Would that help?'

'Oh yes. A single childless man is taxed much more heavily than a married man with a family.' He seemed pleased about it.

'Really?'

'Oh yes.'

'So you are, in fact, fining single childless people.'

He looked at me, suddenly not so pleased. 'Well, that's rather an extreme way . . . '

'If they persist,' I persisted, 'do you put them in prison?'

'What?'

I changed tack slightly. 'I mean, it's a bit hard on people who don't want to get married, isn't it?'

'I think you're overstating the cause.'

'People,' I explained, 'whose sexual inclinations are inappropriate to the institution.'

He worked that one out. He didn't like it.

'I beg your pardon?'

'I mean, *they* could find getting married a problem.' I was thinking of Michael and John, two gay mates of ours who would get married like a shot if they could, and were so bloody happy with each other it was boring.

'I really . . . ' fumbled Hewitson.

'Not to mention getting pregnant.' There again, Michael and John would if they could. It's not as if they don't keep trying, either . . .

'This isn't an aspect . . . ' It was clearly not an aspect that Hewitson had ever considered.

'All this marriage and children . . . ' I sighed. 'It's a bit of a performance, you know. Just to oblige Geoffrey Howe.' It was a nice picture, I thought – couples throughout the length and breadth of Britain, screwing for Sir Geoffrey. Oh well . . .

I changed tack again. 'What if my wife works?'

'Ah.' Firm ground for Hewitson. '*You* are taxed on *her* earnings.'

My turn to work it out. 'So, if my wife earns some money, and doesn't tell me about it, she is, ipso facto, breaking the law?'

'Well . . . yes.'

'Whereas what I earn is between me and the taxman. If I so choose.'

'That's right.'

'So, financially, at any rate, I am more intimate with the taxman than with my wife?'

'Well . . . ' He was out of his depth, and wondering how on

earth I'd managed once again to introduce a sexual note into PAYE.

'Is there anything else?' A genuine question, this. Fun was fun, but somehow I had to win back my hard-earned bread.

'What?'

'I mean, apart from getting married and starting a family, any other little thing I could pop out and do, to ease the situation?'

He looked at my pay slip. 'Well . . . you haven't got a mortgage. You'd get tax relief on that.'

I looked at him, stunned. Mortgage? That's a thing people have when they're middle-aged. Like corns. Or milk stout. Oh well . . .

'How do I get a mortgage then?'

The building society was a little old brick building in the middle of a forest of concrete and glass, and the building society manager was a little old gnome in a forest of con men and sharks. I deliberately chose the local society, rather than one of those monolithic national jobs who are always telling you how big their reserves are. I mean, if they're that big, why don't they use some of it to let poor people buy houses? No, don't tell me. The answer would be too financial to bear.

But the manager was a nice man. An uncle. And when I said I wanted a mortgage he gave me a warm avuncular smile.

'Do you have any savings deposited with the society?' he asked in his kindly way.

'No,' I explained. 'I deposit my money with the Inland Revenue. There's none left over for saving. That's why I want a mortgage.'

'Well . . . ' Regret twinkled in his eye. 'We wouldn't really give you a mortgage if you hadn't saved with the society for a while.'

I stared at him. 'There's a basic flaw in the logic of this.'

He had the grace to look puzzled about it himself. He *was* a nice man.

The next interview was hurried. The man in the registry office was obviously dying for a pint, it being about lunchtime. I was dying for a pint, it being almost any time. Our business did not take long.

'How long would it take to fix up?'

'I'm sorry, Sir?'

'I mean, I've found someone. There'll be no delay there.'

'To fix up what, Sir?'

'To get married.'

The above line is not a misprint. Yes, I was actually in the registry office, enquiring about getting hitched. I must confess that I felt a slight qualm when I left the building. After all, what I was doing was only one step better than marrying a woman for her money. In fact, I was marrying her for *my* money.

What I didn't reckon on, however, was that Fran would say . . .

'No, Shelley.'

'Fran, look . . . '

'No way. *No* way. What'd be the point?'

'But the money . . . '

'Bugger the money!' Inelegant again.

'Fran. Be reasonable.'

'I *am* being reasonable. I will not marry you in a Registry Office. I want the full Church number or nothing.'

Fooled you? Good.

'You're not even Christian,' I told her.

'So what?' She was shameless. 'I'm C of E. If the Church of England had to rely solely on Christians it'd be sharing a room with the Flat Earth Society.'

That made me giggle, which lessened the force of my argument. An old ploy of mine, that. However, I persisted.

'It's such an expense, Fran.'

'My father will pay. He'll be delighted.'

I snorted. 'Your father would rather you married Charles Manson than me.'

Here we went again . . .

'I wish you weren't so prejudiced about Dad.'

'I'm not prejudiced. I just hate him.'

'It's so unreasonable.'

'It's not unreasonable. He hates me.'

'You won't even speak to him.'

'I've got nothing to say to him.'

We paused for breath. Amazing. We'd only just decided to get wed, and already we sounded like an old married couple.

'Tell him about us,' Fran urged. 'That's something.'

I wasn't to be moved. 'You tell him. He's your father.'

'He'll be yours now.'

My God, what a thought.

'Phone him up. Make friends.'

'No Fran.' This was beginning to be a real argument.

'If you want your tax relief . . .'

'*Our* tax relief.'

'Only if you phone him.'

Blackmail! 'You're kidding.'

She wasn't. She folded her arms, pursed her lips, looked ten years older. 'I have every right to expect you to make an effort.'

Shit! I'd lost another bloody argument!

'Gimme the number!'

She passed me the address book. I took it with one hand, and pointed a finger with the other.

'I'd leave you if it wasn't for the child,' I said with force. 'You're lousy in bed, you can't cook, and you don't shave often enough.'

I opened the door. Mrs H. stood there awkwardly. One of her ears was shaped like a keyhole.

'I come to empty the meter.' She looked at me, realised it was no use pretending, and went on. 'Well, she can't be that bad. You're always practising.'

I sketched a courtly bow. 'Do come in, Mrs H.'

'Thank you.' She came. 'You was late leaving again today. You'll lose that job. Don't know what you do in that bathroom.'

Behind her back, I was mouthing the familiar words at Fran, who now had a sudden problem with the giggles.

'If you'll excuse me, Mrs H.,' I announced, 'I have to tell

someone a very important and exciting bit of news.'

Her eyes lit up. 'Who? What news?'

I smiled the smile of the sadist. And slowly closed the door behind me.

TWELVE

IF YOU'VE been paying attention, you will have gathered by now that a certain state of antipathy existed between myself and my lovely lady's horrible old man. Do I mean 'horrible'? Not really. It's just that he and I had nothing in common. That's not entirely true, either. For instance, we both had the same number of feet. But apart from that . . . very little. Indeed, there were times during the following phone conversation when one might be forgiven for wondering whether we spoke the same language.

But at least I made the effort. I was tempted not to. When I closed the door on Mrs H., and made my way downstairs to the phone, I thought about making a run for the pub. But I dismissed that idea almost before it had formed. If I avoided a telephone confrontation with the pompous parent, I'd only have to suffer a face-to-face one with the furious Fran. And when you make a difficult phone call, you can always put the phone down. If I funked it, I had the feeling Fran might put *me* down.

So I made the call. To be strictly accurate, I made several calls. Fran's father lives in a remote country fastness, which possesses a finger-breaking dialling code. I fumbled through the succession of numbers, and was rewarded with, in turn, the engaged tone, the unobtainable tone, a high-pitched buzz, a stroppy wrong number, a series of clicks, an idiot female informing me that lines from Kettering – where? – were engaged, please try later, and then finally, just when I was mentally assigning the P.M.G. to H.E.L.L., the unmistakable brr-brr of a phone ringing out at the other end.

It rang for a long time, until I began to believe that my luck had changed for the better, and he was out. Then, with a clatter, the brr's stopped, and an abrasive voice, indicating in its every tone that I was interrupting work vital to the future of civilisation as we know it, said 'Hello?'

Then the pips began – Mrs H.'s phone is of the thrifty coin-box variety – and I bunged thirty pence in the slot. When the line cleared, the voice was still barking 'hello', and getting nastier every second. Not a good start.

I began carefully. I checked that the speaker was Mr Smith. Yes it was, he said, as if it was totally beyond the realms of possibility that it could be anyone else. So I told him that it was James Shelley speaking.

Of course we had to suffer the usual humorous misunderstanding.

He wanted to know if I was Shelley the poet.

No, I told him, the first name was James.

Not Percy Bysshe?

No. He died in 1822, actually.

People always feel terribly bucked when they go through this one with me. They expect me to be amused. But after twenty years of listening to it, I'm not that enamoured, to be honest.

Instead, in further explanation of who was speaking, I told Mr Smith that I was his daughter's boyfriend.

There was a sound like the last bit of water running out of the bath. Yes, *now* he remembered me.

I kept things civil. I asked after his wife. Silly, that, because I remembered that she'd died five years ago almost as soon as he told me.

I apologised, and enquired after his health. Luckily I remembered his rupture, the result of an accident on Christmas Eve a couple of years ago. His story was he did it while hauling in the traditional Yule Log to burn on the open hearth. I have it on better authority – Fran – that he did it while trying to pull the cork out of a whisky bottle.

But whisky bottles don't have corks!

Exactly.

In answer to my query, Mr Smith told me that his truss was trustworthy, thank you.

I remarked that he must be glad to get back out to do some fox hunting.

Wrong again. Not the thing to say to a prominent member of his local Anti Bloody Sports League. I tried to explain my understandable confusion, but I couldn't, because Mr Smith was busy expressing his understandable outrage. He went on at some length, and the words 'blood' and 'bloody' became as confused as me.

When he came to a halt he had a question of his own. Was it possible that we had met before?

Yes, we had, I admitted. In London.

My God! Now he'd placed me. That time at the ...

Yes, yes. That was me. Ha-ha-ha ...

It wasn't easy, trying to dismiss with a gentle laugh one of the most combative meetings between two men since King Harold met William-the-Thingy. Fran had arranged it with the best intentions. A simple lunchtime pub get-together, it was supposed to be. I remember I had a couple beforehand, to steady my nerves. I expect he did too. We both therefore brought with us a certain fighting spirit. He also brought a friend. She was about thirty, I should guess. No, not her age. Her IQ. She took me for a large gin and vermouth, called me Jimbo, and asked if I was still at school. I kept quiet for a long long time – nearly three minutes on the bar clock – and then I offered a few choice remarks in return. The lady went to the Ladies' in tears, Fran went white at the knuckles, and her dad went bananas. The lady, he informed me, was his intended. Intended for what? I enquired. Then he told me that ...

But why go on? Why recall the pains of yesteryear? Especially when I now had to apologise for it. And apologise I did. I grovelled. I even asked after his ladyfriend's health, and enquired when the wedding would take place.

He wondered what bloody wedding I was talking about, and it slowly transpired that his intended had abandoned him for someone who drove a Ford Granada and sold double-glazing, both of which activities he heartily disapproved.

The conversation, you will have gathered, was not proceeding along the lines that Fran had suggested – that is, acquainting Pater of his daughter's planned nuptials. I decided to get on with it. Indeed, I decided to take the bull by the horns and jump in at the deep end – and if any of you clever clogs out there think I've just mixed my metaphors, you don't know Fran's father.

Mr Smith, I said, I had better tell you exactly why I rang.

A grunt.

It was about Fran, I continued. And indeed, after a little prompting, Mr Smith recalled that he had a daughter called Fran. Splendid. We were getting somewhere.

I now had to tell him that Fran and I had been sharing the same bed and board for some time. Not easy. I told him that we were living . . . well, *close together*, that we had seen a lot of each other, as it were. True, that. Fran has seen bits of me that I've never looked at. But we won't go into that.

Having got this general sort of idea across to him, I wondered aloud if Fran had yet told him about her . . . *news.*

No. She hadn't.

Blast.

She hadn't, I enquired again, said anything to him about the pitter-patter of tiny . . . ?

Mr Smith clearly did not understand the reference. He asked me if insanity was a feature of my family medical history.

At this point the GPO's apparatus began to go blip-blip-blip again. More money needed. I rested the receiver on the box, and shoved thirty pence more in. I looked around, found a chair, pulled it over, sat down. Looked at the receiver. Made familiar digital gestures at it. Picked it up, thought, put it down again, sighed, found thirty pence more, stuck it in the slot, picked up the plastic again, and began.

I didn't um and ah for long. Perhaps ten minutes. I made light of the undeniable fact that Fran had lumbered me with the job of telling him about the big news. Her idea of a joke, ha-ha, and so on.

He told me to get to the bloody point. I got to the bloody point.

He was, I informed him, shortly to become a grandad. And I remembered to say congratulations.

He sounded constricted when he replied. Perhaps he had wrapped his end of the telephone wire around his own neck. Did I mean that his daughter was pregnant? Well, yes, I did. She was going to have a . . .

He made a suggestion. He made it forcibly, and it was not a pleasant suggestion. No, I'm not saying what it was. Suggestions of that sort have no place in a work of taste and refinement such as this, and if I did relate his exact proposal it would only get the sadists amongst you excited.

I'll just say that I informed him that this particular method of disposing of people had been abolished round about 1172, and had been replaced by the infinitely more humane method known as hanging, drawing and quartering.

It didn't stop him. Steam hissed out of my receiver. He suggested an alternative course of action which was more simple, yet not less terrifying, and I had to agree that it would certainly prevent me from fathering any *more* children, but . . .

He continued with this theme for some time, and there was quite a lot more about what he would and wouldn't do to me, before I was able to break in and try to make things better.

When that moment came, I stuttered out the intelligence that before Mr Smith became a grandad, he would indeed become a dad-in-law.

A short but deathly silence. Then – did I mean that Fran and . . . *me* were going to . . .

Yes, I did. He would be my dad-in-law! Hello Dad! Ha-ha-ha. My jovial chuckle clattered down the wires, and probably frightened millions of starlings.

Mr Smith's next few words were rather difficult to catch. That happens when you bellow down a phone. I gathered he had a certain basic objection to his daughter marrying a no-good idle useless bloody layabout. I think he meant me.

I protested. I was not a layabout any more. Yes, I had been a layabout, perhaps. Even, I would agree, a fairly useless example of same.

But . . .

Mr Smith apparently did not like layabouts. Hanging was

too good for 'em. He'd do it. He'd pull the lever. He'd swing on their ankles. Etcetera, etcetera. Well, he was upset.

I told him that now I worked for a living. And the tide, for a moment, was, if not turned, at least stemmed.

So I went ahead and broke the really bad news. His daughter wanted a full Church wedding, all the trimmings, so would he please cough up the cash.

What was wrong with a registry office, he'd like to know. So would I, was my reaction.

That was wrong too. Was I denying his daughter her rightful and proper wedding ceremony? No no no, heaven forbid, I wouldn't dream of any other sort of wedding.

By now I had a headache. I had been verbally battered and bruised. Indeed, I had not taken such a wordy beating since the day Miss Fortescue actually caught me putting my hand up Beryl Wilson's skirt. Why was I suffering like this? I asked myself. Because I love Fran, was the answer. But did she not love me? And if she did, why wasn't she standing side by side with me, sharing this moment of trial? After all, he was *her* flipping father . . .

I suggested to Mr Smith that really Fran should be telling him all this herself. But, ha-ha-ha, she'd made me do it, ho-ho-ho, he knew how stubborn she could be, he-he-he.

No, he didn't know how stubborn she could be. He couldn't imagine what I meant. He was very stubborn about it.

I told him I'd go and fetch her, now that I had put him in the picture. He grunted. I told him how much I'd enjoyed chatting to him. Another grunt. I suggested we might meet soon. Silence. Oh well . . . Bye bye, Mr Smith . . .

I let the receiver dangle, and got up from the chair. My legs trembled as I climbed the stairs.

Modern doors are made of two ultra-thin sheets of boarding, with nothing between them. Someone like Mrs Hawkins can be heard through such a door, without resource to the ear-'ole to the key-'ole method.

'Eh, 'ang on, warrabout a wedding dress?' my landlady wanted to know. It was clear that Fran had told her about our plans. For the umpteenth time I wondered why those two got along so well. ' 'Ere!' Mrs H. sounded almost shocked. 'You're never going to wear white in your condition!'

I opened the door. 'No, Mrs H. It's going to be West Hampstead's first nude wedding!'

'You're kidding!' She wasn't sure. She wouldn't put anything past me.

I looked over her head at Fran. 'Genghis Khan would like a word with you.'

'Shelley!'

'Who?' from Mrs H.

'Did you tell him we're getting married?' Fran asked anxiously.

'Yes, I did.'

'Thank God.' She cheered up considerably. 'Well done. It'll be much easier now.'

'What will?'

'To tell him I'm pregnant.'

'Ah.' Good grief! I'd gone all through that for nothing! Conscience pricked me, too. I'd been hard on Fran. I might have known she wouldn't intentionally leave me all the dirty work. Serve me right.

Fran went off to the phone, leaving Mrs H. and I alone. Mrs H. was still obsessed with the wedding.

'It's never going to be a nood wedding, don't talk rubbish. Is it?'

I grinned. 'Worried about where to put your carnation, Mrs H.?'

She actually blushed. 'You're rude, you are.'

'You're taking it very well, Mrs H.'

' 'Ere . . . ' Another puzzle . . . 'Who's this Dennis Khan?'

I put a comforting arm around her thin shoulders. 'Anything you want, Mrs H.? Sweet tea? Biscuit? Quick lay-down?'

She punched me, not too hard, in the ribs. 'You're a lucky devil! I can't see what she sees in you.'

Fran came back in before I could tell her.

'Got any tens, love? The money's run out.'

Mrs H. decided she'd had enough of being left alone with me. 'I'm orf. Congratulations on your news. I'm very 'appy for you.' She looked as happy as a walrus. 'Thanks for the tea.'

I waited until she'd gone. Then – 'I told your father you were pregnant.'

'You cretin!' Quite correct, really.

'I thought I was supposed to. I thought . . . '

'You dumbo!' Not inaccurate, you must admit.

'I got confused, you see.'

Fran saw, all right. She grinned. 'What did he say?'

I don't believe in using bad language in front of women. These days they only use it back at you. So I prevaricated.

'Well, he's an articulate man, with a comprehensive vocabulary, and . . . '

Fran thought for a moment. 'I think I'll phone him later,' she decided. Wise girl.

'However,' I went on, 'his enthusiasm for the wedding was unbounded.'

'Was it?'

'Oh yes. I don't suppose he's that bad really.'

A sigh. 'Don't pretend, Shelley.'

'Sorry.' We'd been unmarried too long, she knew me too well. 'He's just not really my type of man.'

'No, I know. Not mine either.'

I felt we could forget about Daddy for a while.

'Before the conversation turns to what we're going to do tonight,' I began, 'there's no money.' So no films or theatres.

'What?'

I ticked them off on my fingers, 'Tax, rent, building society.'

That last one shocked her. 'What?'

'Investment. For the mortgage.' It sounded strange to say those words. 'It's been rather a significant sort of day,' I added.

'Oh no!' She was really disappointed. She wanted her new film.

'Sorry.' So was I.

'Shelley, we're getting married,' said Fran with frustration. 'We must do *something* to celebrate.'

Well . . . we did. We did what I wanted to do, early that morning.

Better than films, isn't it!

THIRTEEN

FRAN DID ring her father back, later on. And soon there were plans afoot for us to visit him where he lives, deep in rural Britain and up to his elbows in muck and pheasants. It was clear that, no matter how much he and I disliked each other, we were destined to be thrust together time and again in the future. It's all part of marriage, I suppose. And, like the poor, parents are always with us. While we suffer them, perhaps all we can do in return is to make life equally bloody for our own children.

Meanwhile there were other things to do. It occurred to me that if I was to suffer the formal indignity of a public Church mating, I would require a so-called 'best man'. Unlike the registry office ceremony, for which one just calls in the nearest two strangers off the street to act as witnesses, a real 'best man' should at least be on speaking terms with the bridegroom. Preferably he should be a friend who can be trusted, someone for whom one has respect. Which is why it's often more difficult to select a best man than it is to select a bride.

For me it came down to a choice between two. One was Laurence, who would have turned the whole ceremony into a publicity stunt for himself. The other was Ned.

Ned is my boyhood friend and my manhood mate. He's not a respectable friend. He's the boy my mother told me not to play with. He knew about sex and babies when I was still learning about tadpoles. When we pulled two birds at the school dance, I got the ugly one. He's the Huckleberry Finn in my life, and I love him. I must do. If I didn't, what follows would not have happened. I would not have had a row with Fran. I would not have got involved in a punch-up. I would not have wandered the corridors of Charing Cross Hospital late at night. The truth is that Raymond 'Ned' Kelly holds a position in my life of irresistible influence, and my only consolation is, I hold a similar position in his.

The position we both held on a Friday evening at about seven-thirty was the traditional one: right elbow at ninety degrees to the chest, right hand gripping pint-pot, eyes closed in anticipation of ecstasy.

We were in The Red Lion. The Red Lion is a real pub, selling real beer, for real beer drinkers. From where we sat, at a corner table, the long bar stretched away across the room, a shining board dotted with formations of traditional beer pumps. On these pumps were clipped some of the famous names in beer – Young's, Marston's, Ruddles – and the place was crowded with big men and big girls sinking big pints. There was a slight air of heartiness – the fate of many real ale bars, sad to say – but Ned and I ignored the berks and concentrated on the brews. We raised our glasses of Burper's Old and Terrible Ale, and we drank. A quarter of a pint of liquid magic slipped down the inside of each throat.

Ned put his glass back down on the table, and looked at it critically.

'What do you think?' he asked.

'Not a lot,' I said airily.

'No.' He lit a cigarette. 'I know what you mean.'

'It's past its best,' I pontificated.

'Lacks bite,' he considered.

'Over sweet,' I judged.

'Too warm,' he suggested.

'Unsubtle flavour,' I opined.

'No body,' he reflected.

We picked up our glasses again.

'Apart from that . . .'

'Nectar!'

Another quarter of a pint slid down to join the first.

Much of our conversation was like the above – often designed to confuse and irritate a third party. In-jokes, past experiences, identical senses of humour, all combined to form a kind of code, and there was no way an outsider could break it. If Fran had been with us, she would not have been happy.

There was a crash of glass up at the bar. Some hearty laughter. A drunk had misjudged the strength of Greene King Abbott, and was making a fool of himself. I didn't blame him. It might have been me. Good God, many times in the past it *had* been me.

I waved a hand at the clumps of pumps.

'Have you ever, at one sitting, gone through the lot?' I asked Ned.

'Not since lunchtime.'

'Seriously.'

He shrugged. 'No time like the present.'

Ned meant it. Ten or twelve pints – that was hardly his idea of a binge. More of a staple diet. I don't know where he put it all, he was so slight and thin. Look at him from north to south and he was hardly there. Pipe-cleaner-man, I used to call him. I watched as he had another belt at his pint, and lit a second ciggie from the end of the first. He wheezed. Of course, it would help if he would eat.

Another crash of breaking glass. They call the strong beers 'idiot soup', and it was on the menu tonight. Crash, again. Not so much laughter this time. Then a stool fell over.

'God, it's noisy in here tonight.'

Ned breathed grey smoke, and looked around the bar with red-rimmed eyes. 'Mmmm. I knew this place when you could have a really quiet drink.'

'Now it's like the House of Commons.'

As I watched, a particularly big 'hearty', who had been in the centre of the glass-breakers, now casually leaned across the wide bar, and hit the barman with the full sweep of his open hand. The man toppled like a skittle, crashing over a crate of empty bottles before hitting the floor. He lay still. He was a bit old for that sort of thing.

'Hello,' I alerted Ned. 'Spot of bother.'

Ned sucked his teeth in resignation. 'Not good.'

We watched. A small man now approached the drunken gorilla. I recognised him as the landlord. Good luck, mate, I thought grimly. He needed it – but one had the feeling he wasn't going to get it. He spoke to the drunk, who responded to the manner born by deliberately and roughly pushing the landlord in the chest. Surrounding cronies thought that was funny. Ned sighed, buttoned up his denim jacket, and made to rise.

'I don't like violence, Ned,' I told him.

'Well . . . no.' He sat back.

'I mean,' I explained, 'I've got this thing about being physically assaulted.'

'How do you mean?'

'I'm a coward.'

'Aaah!' Ned looked back at the scene by the bar. It was not improving. Thug-features now had the landlord by both lapels, and was shaking him.

'We could take him,' Ned reckoned.

'Yes,' I agreed, reasonably. 'Or we could run. Or buy him a drink. Or hold the other bloke down for him.'

Ned looked at me, just a trifle critically. 'But he's a violence-loving intolerant Fascist thug. Everything you hate.'

I tried to keep things light. 'But you've got to say one thing for him.'

'What?'

'He's big.'

I offered a casual laugh, but Ned wasn't having any of it. 'So are you, Jim.'

'Oh no.' I shook my head. 'Lots of people make that mistake. I only *look* big. People *think* I'm big. Inside I'm tiny.'

The bully at the bar knocked the landlord down. Some girl screamed. Helpful. The landlord tried to get up, and had his legs kicked from under him. Oh dear oh dear . . .

'We cannot stand by and let this happen.' Ned used the formal phrase in self-mockery, but he was quite serious. He, at least, could not stand by and let this happen. What about me?

'Try me,' I suggested.

'Jim!' He looked at me, reproachfully. He knew that where

he led, I would follow. I nodded, to confirm it. Bloody hell, we were going to be in a fight. Bloody hell!

Ned moved off with purpose towards the bar. I stood up, finished my beer with one swallow, and started after him. I was terrified.

What happened then is a bit blurry, to be honest. I do remember that Ned's participation in the scrimmage lasted for as long as it took the trouble-maker to stick out one fist in the direction of his face. As I said, he's a spindly little chap. So from then on he was just a rather light dead-weight, receiving the occasional kick as he rolled in the broken glass. Me, I did my cowardly best. I struck out manfully, and managed to catch the big chap a very nasty blow on the fist with my nose. A little later I found myself outside the pub and inside a telephone kiosk, bleeding copiously down the phone at the police. A wagon came and took the hooligan away, and an ambulance came and took Ned away. They wouldn't let me come. They assured me he was okay, and just needed a check-over. I trusted they were right. To me he looked terrible. I felt extremely sorry for him, and extremely sorry for myself, and I went home to Fran.

The one thing you can rely on getting from Fran is a realistic reaction.

'So, how come you got off so lightly?'

Charming. 'I ran.'

'Shelley – you didn't!'

I nodded. My head ached. 'Phoned the police. Look, this guy was the Incredible Hulk's Big Brother, and he *enjoyed* hitting people.' I had another thought. 'He was probably Australian.'

Sorry about that gratuitous insult to you chaps from Down Under. I do realise that many Australian men thoroughly resent being described as violent, and they hit anyone who tries it.

'Surely the landlord had phoned the police?' Fran suggested.

'The landlord was laid out.' But not badly, thank heaven. No hospital for him.

'You left Ned there?'

'Well . . . ' I hadn't exactly *left* him. Had I?

'I mean, he's so tiny, Shelley.'

'He's wiry,' I told her. 'He's also determined. He was making things worse . . . ' This didn't help. 'Look,' I went on, 'I'm a coward, that's it. I make no secret of it. If you're being beaten up in a dark alley, and the only passer-by is a crippled old lady, you're out of luck. Likewise if it's me. Except the old lady's probably got a better left hook than I have. I'm just no good as a fighter. My eyes were ruined as a kid.'

That got to her. 'Eh?'

'By all the sand that was kicked in my face,' I explained.

'Where's Ned now?'

'Charing Cross Hospital.'

'Still?'

'They're just doing some tests.' I'd checked by phone. 'He's all right.'

Fran sighed, got up, went out to the kitchen and started banging things about. A sign that she had something specific to say. Funny, that.

I waited, and finally she came to the door and said it, 'Every time you go out with that man, something happens.'

'Yeah.' I smiled with happy reflection. 'He's all right, is Ned.'

'Hmmm.' Lot of meaning in it.

I sighed. 'What?'

'Nothing.'

'*What?*' I wasn't in the mood for playing games.

'Well . . . ' And then it came. 'I just don't like him very much.'

I was honestly surprised. 'You never said.'

'No, well . . . '

'Ah!' I was struck by a nasty thought. 'That's a bit awkward.'

'What?'

'I asked him to be best man.'

'You did what?' As if she hadn't heard!

'I asked him,' I said helplessly.

Fran gave me that look – a mixture of exasperation and determination – that you give to a puppy when the house-training doesn't take.

'Shelley, I'm not having that man . . . '

'He said,' I put in heavily, 'it was the best thing that ever happened to him. He's over the moon. He can't wait.'

'But . . .'

'And it *is* my choice,' I insisted. 'Groom's best friend. That's the rules. Besides, I need someone on my side to balance your father.'

You'd think I'd know better by now, wouldn't you, Fran had been fuming inwardly. Now, at the mention of her father, she fumed outwardly.

'Have you thought what'll happen when my father meets Ned?'

I hadn't, but I did now. 'He'll have to go into an intensive care unit.' I was snorting with laughter. 'He thinks Keith Joseph is a bit of a Lefty – and Ned's a card-carrying member of the Workers' Revolutionary Party!' The prospect was hysterical.

'Shelley!' Fran didn't find it at all amusing. 'The best man gives a speech at the reception!'

Oh boy! Further visions of nihilism at the nuptials. 'It'll be a party political. He'll pass round pictures of Vanessa Redgrave. He'll call them Comrades!'

By now I was rocking back and forth on the chair at my own merriment. It took Fran's coldest eye and most rigid pose to stop me.

'I don't find it funny, Shelley.'

I looked at her. No, she didn't find it funny. Not one little bit.

'No, no, I'm sorry . . . ' I'd dug myself in pretty deep, it was going to be tricky climbing out. 'I'm sorry, it's just . . . well, he is my best friend. He's a great bloke. I'm sorry you don't like him. He's done a lot for me, over the years.'

I looked up at her. She wasn't impressed. I felt the usual tide of guilt sweeping me off my feet.

'Well . . . ' I was giving in again. 'I'll see what I can do.'

'Can I help you?'

Could she help me? Yes, she most certainly could!

'She' was a ward sister at Charing Cross Hospital, and she was part of the new hospital policy towards ward sisters. As you doubtless know, it used to be the rule that no hospital management committee could appoint a ward sister unless she was old, scrawny, ugly, and unpleasant. Then, much as happens in Chinese politics, there was a coup within the National Health Service, and a totally new and radical policy towards ward sisters was promulgated. This policy is still in force today, and it rules that ward sisters should be aged between thirty and forty, and be warm, cuddly, generous, and nice, with just that touch of firmness and competence that turns them into every young lad's ideal of the sexy older woman. Result – being ill is getting popular. It's even fun – at least, it would be fun to be here in Ned's ward, with this ward sister. I looked at her, at her dark glowing cheeks and her dark bouncy hair, and, undoubtedly beneath that crisp uniform, her dark bouncy bosom, and I was tempted to plead a suspected hernia and ask for an immediate bed-bath.

Instead I muttered, 'I wondered if I could see Mr Kelly. Mr Raymond Kelly.'

'Well . . . ' She gave me a look that was both severe and accommodating. Par for the course. 'It's not visiting time . . . '

Behind her, working at some kind of register, was a nurse. Fanciable, too. But I kept my eyes on Sister, and threw myself upon her boundless bosom . . . sorry, I mean, mercy.

'You see, I'm an international lorry driver, only just got in, and I leave tonight for Tehran. Won't be back for a month.'

She didn't believe a word of this. She wasn't really supposed to.

'And you're . . . ?'

'Shelley. Jim Shelley.'

'Are you a relative?'

'Well, we shared a double desk all the way to O-level.'

I smiled at her. She smiled at me. Told me to wait, then disappeared.

'That must be an exciting job.' That was the nurse, who was looking quite interested.

'Hmmm?' What the . . . ? Oh yes. Tehran. 'Yes, you get about, you know.'

'What are you taking to Tehran?'

'Um . . . ' Quick now, think of something. 'It's a pilot load of dralon yashmaks. Part of the export drive.'

'Good Lord!'

This surprised her nearly as much as it had surprised me.

'What do you bring back?'

Oh, hell . . . 'Um . . . well . . . tell you the truth – escaped political prisoners.'

'You're joking!'

'No. The yashmaks are just a cover. I'm a hit man for Amnesty International.' I was getting into my stride. 'I don't suppose you'd care to make a donation?'

That's where it stopped, and just as well. Sister reappeared, smiled, and beckoned. 'Mr Shelley?'

'Ah, thanks.' I made for the ward entrance door.

'Don't be *too* long,' she called.

'Don't worry. The lorry's double-parked.'

And there, in the end bed, was my mate Ned. He looked dreadful. Huckleberry Thin. Weary, battered, even old. I'd been wrong. It is never fun to be ill.

FOURTEEN

'JIM! HELLO mate! Pull up a drip feed and sit down!'

That was a relief – the same chirpy Ned, eyes bright in the pallid face.

I stood awkwardly by the bed. 'I've . . . um . . . I've donated the kidney, Ned.'

'Aw Jim, you shouldn't have.'

'They've got it in pathology.'

Ned was lucky. They'd given him an end bed in the ward. End beds are a hospital luxury, because if you're in one, and you lie on one side, you can sometimes kid yourself that you're enjoying the barest minimum of privacy. Of course, it takes a vivid imagination, especially when someone just behind you is hawking his lungs up and depositing them bit by bit in a plastic cup. Oh well . . .

Mind you, Ned was particularly lucky with this bed. The one next to him was screened off, presumably because whoever occupied it was either dead or about to be. And in the bed opposite an extremely old chap was rather noisily asleep. Result – he and I could talk our usual bilge without being overheard.

'Blimey, Ned, you look terrible!' Shelley's best bedside manner.

Ned grinned. 'Gerraway.'

'No, straight up. It's quite an effort to look at you. You look like you just died. How d'you feel?'

'Well, a bit seedy,' he admitted.

'Bloody hell, I'm glad it's not me mate, I can tell you.'

'Knock it off, Jim!'

'Calm down, Ned. Easy. Easy now. That's it.' I took a fresh Kleenex from a box on his locker, and did the Doctor Kildare bit on his forehead. 'Sister said you're not to get excited. Spot of bad news I'm afraid, Ned.'

'Wassat?'

'They've spelt your name wrong on the danger list.'

'What've they called me?' Ned came back. 'Dead Kelly?'

'Now, now, we mustn't talk like that. You've got hours in front of you yet.'

You may think I'd gone slightly loopy with all the death jokes. But I know my Ned. He was already brightening under the influence of such black humour.

'They're still trying to contact your next of kin,' I went on. 'Radio Four are giving you a smashing SOS. You get top billing, with the Nolan Sisters singing "Abide With Me" in the background.'

Ned laughed out loud, then punched me gently on the arm. 'Listen, Jim, thanks for coming. You needn't have bothered.'

'Course I came!' I went babbling on, partly because I sensed from his last remark that Ned wanted something from me. 'Probably be my last chance to come, this. They've done out these terminal wards nicely, haven't they!'

'Jim – I want you to do something for me.'

See? I was right. I decided to ignore him for the moment.

'So why are you here, eh? Worrying David Ennals half to death like this. You weren't hit that hard.'

'They ran a few routine tests.'

'And?'

'I failed them all.'

'Typical!' And worrying, but I kept my mouth shut about that. 'So what do they say?'

He grinned. 'They keep asking me how much I drink.'

'Aha!'

'And I say, you know, roundabout eleven or twelve pints a day.'

'Well, you have to knock some off, don't you? Save worrying them.'

'Exactly,' Ned agreed. He lit a cigarette, coughed, then said rather aptly, 'Apparently there's enough tar in my lungs to do a mile of the M1. So then they ask me what food I eat.'

I gave him a sideways look. 'You don't do *that*, do you?'

'Well, this is it. I told him, I never touch the stuff. Bad for you, all this obesity, it's the number one killer, they've got commercials about it.'

Funny. But Ned really does under-eat to excess. He's been known to dine exclusively off the little white bits you sometimes find at the bottom of a pint of real ale.

'So then,' he continued, 'we have the blood tests.' He adopted the voice of a jovial doctor. 'I daren't let anything happen to you, Mr Kelly, or the shareholders of Allied Breweries will lynch me.'

'Oh, ho-ho-ho' – ironic laughter from me.

Ned tried another line in his 'doctor' voice. 'I won't take a lot, because we have to pay duty on it.'

'He sounds terrific.'

'Oh yeah. We have all the jokes.'

I tried one myself. 'My car would do ninety to the gallon on this.'

Ned – 'This is what I call a real Bloody Mary.'

Me – 'We can only take your blood during licensing hours.'

Ned – 'You ought to be in a bonded warehouse, not a hospital.'

And that was enough for us. We both yawned hugely. I reckoned I was doing my bit in cheering up the patient. And myself. Then Ned put the bite on.

'Anyway, Jim, this is where you come in.'

'They don't want my blood, do they?'

'No, look, see, they want a urine test off me.'

So what, I wondered. 'People are always taking that out of you, Ned.'

He ignored the cheap crack. 'Look, the bottle's in the cabinet there. I wondered if you'd oblige.'

'What?' I sat down on the side of the bed rather suddenly. 'You kidding?' He wasn't. I could tell.

'No,' he said seriously. 'I reckon yours is better than mine.'

Jesus! I got up again, and walked about a bit. 'Look – that's got to be the ultimate inferiority complex.'

Ned shook his head. 'No. You see, they asked me to cut out the drinking. And . . .'

'And?'

Wordlessly, Ned opened his locker. I looked in. Good grief! He only had a minipin of Fuller's London Pride in there. Complete with gas tap.

'See?' He grinned up at me. 'I'll lose my licence.'

Sometimes Ned is almost too much. One thing I knew for certain, he was not going to get a pint of my pee. There had to be another way around this.

'Couldn't you discharge yourself?'

'Oh no.' So self-righteous. 'Not until I've been cleared.'

'Well . . . look, I'm probably the wrong group.'

He shook his head. 'It's not like that, Jim.'

'I know. I'm stalling for time.'

'Why?'

' 'Cos I'm horrified by this flouting of authority.' That was rich, coming from me.

'Hospitals aren't authority.'

'Course they are.' I was thinking rapidly. I could feel myself being driven into a corner. It's not as if I didn't want to help Ned. Only . . .

'Look, if I perform for you, it'll confuse their diagnosis, and maybe you've got some dreadful . . . ' Oh dear. The bedside manner again. 'I mean, I'm sure you haven't, but *if* you have, they won't find out about it.'

Ned nodded. 'That's it.'

'What is?'

'Well – I must be ill.'

'Why?'

'You try subsisting on draught beer and cigarettes for ten years.'

Very reasonable. 'Well, there you are,' I told him.

'Yes, but I'm not *suffering* from it. But if they *find* it, and give it a name, they'll slap me in an oxygen tent, and have a team of priests standing by on double-time.'

'Ned!' He wasn't being logical. I gave him my most reproachful look.

'I know, Jim, I know.' He was, of course, beaten. The plain fact was, he should have his own urine analysed. But Ned is not the sort of weakling who lets a mere fact change his mind.

'I want them to check me out,' he went on. 'I just don't want to upset them – you know? I'll lay off the booze tomorrow.'

'Ho-ho-ho.' Fat chance.

'Jim! All I want is a half pint of Jimmy Riddle. It's not much to ask for. I mean, you weren't going to do anything special with it, were you?'

What did he think I was – an Indian Prime Minister? 'Look, Ned . . .'

He held up a skinny hand. 'Jim, what are the three answers to this question: Will you lend me a fiver?'

I sighed. I knew where this would get me. I'd made it up myself. 'Yes, No, and What's It For,' I told him.

'And what's the worst of those answers?'

Another sigh. 'What's It For?'

'Lend me half a pint of Jimmy Riddle. I'll pay you back whenever you want.'

'No!' I'm clutching at straws now.

'That's the second worst answer,' Ned told me. 'We're getting nearer. I'm your best friend. We love each other deeply. We have shared magic experiences behind the bike sheds of a nature not to be discussed in mixed company.'

He would bring that up. It was just two chaps finding out about themselves. Quite natural and normal. Still makes me blush, though.

'That's just a phase, Ned. Everyone . . .' I began. But Ned was not about to let me off.

'There have been occasions when I've been of some small assistance to you, in times of need.' He looked me in the eyes. '*Please* will you lend me . . . ?'

I could have copped out. I could have said 'no', justifying my decision on the grounds of Ned's health and welfare. But life is meaningless if you keep saying 'no' to someone you love. The hell with it, I copped in.

'Where's the bottle?'

'That's the best answer,' Ned congratulated me. 'Top shelf.'
'And where do I do the deed?' I asked.
'Eh?'
'Well, I can't just stand up here, can I? It's rude.'
'You could. Close in to the bed. No one'll see you.'
'They'll listen!'
Ned sighed. 'There's a gents in the corridor.'
I marched out, bottle behind back, sidled past the reception desk – nurse still there but no sign of Sister – and dived into the Gents'. It was small, hospital-clean and empty. I went into one of the cubicles, uncapped bottle, unzipped equipment . . . and waited. One minute turned into two. Nothing. I thought of waterfalls, I thought of torrents and deluges, I pressed the flush handle, and finally, way back down deep in the waterworks, something stirred. And in due time, sweating with the effort, I eventually produced an amber sufficiency. And so then, there I was, toddling out of the Gents' with pride in my heart and a little warm bottle in my hand, and standing right outside the door as if she'd been waiting for me, was Sister.
'I'll take that, Mr Shelley.'
'What?' I tried to hide the bottle. Too late.
'That. I'm going to microbiology.'
'Ah, no, you see . . . ' Oh Gawd!
She smiled. 'I didn't know that's why you were here.'
'No, no, I came to see Ned, Mr Kelly . . . '
'Ah, two birds with one stone! Jolly good. Do you have your card?'
What? 'No. No. No . . . no. In fact . . . '
She gave me a sort of roguish grin and waved an admonitory finger. 'If you knew how many people lose those.'
'Well . . . I haven't. Actually.'
She led me firmly over to the reception desk, took the full bottle from me, and plonked it on the counter.
'I'll make one out now. What's your doctor's name?'
'Frobisher, but this isn't mine,' I babbled.
'I beg your pardon?'
'Um . . . this isn't mine.'
'Are you carrying it round for a friend?'
'Um . . . no . . . you see . . . '

'Who's is it?'

'Well . . . ' I was not going to drop Ned in the urine.

'You went in there with it empty, and now it's full. If it isn't yours, what did you do? Take up a collection?'

I was on the ropes and staggering. The referee should have stepped in and stopped the fight. I was taking unnecessary punishment.

'Um . . . you see . . . ' I pointed at the card she was now filling out. 'Um . . . Doctor Frobisher . . . '

'Initial?'

'L. Laurence. And what happened . . . '

'His address?'

I gave it. 'But you see, all it was, slight touch of the old complaint, nothing.'

'That's not my concern, Mr Shelley.'

'No no, of course not, but . . . '

'Your address?'

I gave that too. 'But you see, it's all cleared up now, I shouldn't have bothered him in the first place, I think I'll just forget it, you know.'

'But your doctor has requested a urine test.'

What? My God . . . 'Has he?' Then I realised. That's what *I* was saying. If you see what I mean. My head was beginning to hurt. 'Oh, I see. Yes. Yes, he has. In a way . . . '

'Well, I presume he has, Mr Shelley.' She's ultra-smooth now. To think that once I liked her! 'You've come all the way from West Hampstead with a specimen bottle which you've just filled, I take it that wasn't just because you felt at a bit of a loose end.'

'Oh no . . . no.'

I wanted to cry. She was going for the kill now. The crowd – if there'd been a crowd – were roaring her on. Everything was going black before my eyes. I made myself a silent and solemn vow that nothing ever again in my entire life would induce me to pee in anything other than a loo.

Sister bore in. 'Has your doctor requested it, or not?'

I threw in the towel. 'Yes. Mmm. Yes. Yes, he asked, you know, if I'd . . . if I'd . . . and I did.'

'Fine.' Glowing smile. Wonderful teeth. No wonder they'd

chewed me to ribbons. 'Well, he should have the result in a couple of days.'

I tried to look pleased about it. 'Terrific. Smashing. Thanks a lot. Be nice to know. One way or the other. You know . . . been a bit worried. Thanks for your help.'

'You're welcome.' Another big smile. Something fishy here. 'Are you going back to see Mr Kelly?'

'Well, if you don't mind . . . '

'I wonder if you'd be good enough to give him this.' She produced another specimen bottle, empty. 'He seems to have lost his.'

I took it. But she held on to it for a few moments, her firm fingers warm against mine, her gold wedding ring gleaming. She pulled slightly, brought us closer together, and I looked deep down into her lustrous brown eyes. I felt slightly giddy.

'Tell him . . . ' she said, and somewhere in the depths there was a brilliant sparkle, 'Tell him all we want is half a pint of Jimmy Riddle.'

She knew! She'd known all along. All the time I'd been stammering and stuttering about my miserable little bottle of pee, she'd probably been in danger of producing some herself, due to internal laughter. My God – wasn't she something?

I decided on reflection that it must have been that bed next to Ned's, the one screened off. She must have been in there for some reason, shaving someone or sharpening the enemas, or something. She'd heard everything we'd said. Everything.

I told Ned what had happened. I felt very silly. Then I went home and told Fran. I felt even sillier.

'What did Ned say?' Fran asked.

'You know Ned,' I told her. 'He took it philosophically. Swore at me for fifteen minutes solid, chucked his tablet bottle at me, turned "The Archers" full on. But it's okay now. I guess he'll even speak to me in a month or two.'

'What a man!' There was no admiration in Fran's tone, and that irritated me.

'I can't think why you hate him. He's such a nice guy.'

'Oh, I don't hate him!' We were having a meal in an Asian

restaurant – belated celebration of my entry into the salary-earning classes – and she put her knife and fork down and reached across to put a hand on my arm.

'I don't hate him. In fact. I quite like him, to tell you the truth. It's you two Butch Cassidy and the Sundance Kidding all over the place I can't stand. I feel so excluded. It's you, Ned, and sixty tons of machismo.'

I knew what she meant. 'What do you mean?' I asked.

She sighed. 'Well – you've done things I can't share.'

My God! She knew about the bike sheds! 'How did you find out about that?'

'About what?'

Another thought hit me below the belt. If the ward sister knew about the Jimmy Riddle, then she also knew about the bike sheds. Oh dear . . .

'You been talking to that ward sister?' I asked Fran.

'Eh?'

'Ned wouldn't tell you.'

'Shut up, Shelley.'

I shut up, and looked at Fran. Her attitude towards Ned had indeed changed, I felt. But not enough. She still didn't want a drunken anarchist best man turning her wedding into a violent political shambles. Can't blame her, can you? And yet Ned was so keen. Oh . . . God damn and blast it! I'd have to tell him.

'What'll they do for Ned?' Fran asked.

'Well, they want to change his diet a bit. Substitute food for drink. Try to get him down to a pound of tobacco a day.'

'How'll they do that?'

'Break him in gently.' I grinned. 'Whisk an egg into his breakfast pint. Get him to nibble something after a good smoke.'

Fran laughed. 'Why are they so sure he's ill.'

'The very fact he's alive at all is a challenge to present-day medical knowledge.'

'Well . . . it's down to him then, isn't it?' Logical, of course. But a little hard. 'Did he really expect you to fill his bottle?'

'Certainly.'

'But why? He either stays in and is treated, or he discharges himself.'

'Oh, he wouldn't discharge himself,' I explained. 'He wouldn't want to be rude to the doctors. No, it's a peasant mentality – get out, but get out clean.'

Fran thought about this for a moment. She forked an onion ball into her mouth, then nodded at my plate.

'What have you got there, Shelley?'

'Um . . . ' I looked at it, identified it. 'Roast chicken and two veg. It's quite nice actually.'

'You're worried about Ned, aren't you?'

A penetrating non-sequitur, I had to admit. 'What makes you say that?'

'You ordered Mutton Doupiaza with pilau rice.'

FIFTEEN

NEXT DAY I returned to Ned's ward. Super-Sister was waiting for me at the entrance. My first instinct, given my natural courage and spirit, was to turn around and run away. But I took a deep breath, and sailed up to her, looking confident and relaxed. Inside I was about as relaxed as an electric eel.

However, I got in the first word.

'You eavesdropped, Miss Nightingale.'

She gave a slight bow. 'You lied, Mr Shelley.'

'Yes.' I wondered to which lie she referred. The pantomime with the pee bottle? Or the lorry driver bullshit? I chose to believe it was the latter.

'Yes, I lied. In order to see my best friend, with whom I have a close and special relationship.'

'Cemented behind the bike sheds,' she said. At least, I think she said 'cemented'.

I nodded gravely. 'In California we'd have got married.'

'In California your urine test would have cost you thirty dollars!'

I knew we'd get round to the pee bottle.

'I'm glad you mentioned that.' Lying again. 'I don't actually want . . .'

'I know.' A brief smile. 'I phoned Dr Frobisher.' Then came the censorious bit. 'If people behaved responsibly, Mr Shelley, the Health Service would be saved a great deal of money.'

This time I bowed to her. 'I'd love to stay and chat about your political ideology, but my desk-mate beckons. Bye!'

I gave her a little wave, and escaped into the ward.

Ned was squatting on his bed, wearing one sock and a big smile. Thank God – he no longer looked at death's door. During the night he'd retreated a little down death's garden path.

'Jim!' he cried, with the happiness of the reprieved prisoner. 'I got off with a caution.'

'Yeah?'

'Right! They couldn't pin it on me. They had the best specialists in the country. One of them was a QC. But they couldn't make it stick.'

Ned's well-being was . . . well, it was infectious. 'Absolute discharge?' I asked.

'Unconditional. They've got to burn me X-rays.' He motioned me closer with a jerk of his head, then hissed, 'They got the bloke on the end, though.'

'Yeah?' I looked down the ward. In the far end bed a pale figure lay motionless.

'Badly beaten up,' Ned gritted.

'Resisting treatment, eh?'

'Right.'

'Fell off his bed, I expect. So what did he get?'

'Six colonic irrigations, without the option.'

We both sucked our teeth in grim sympathy. As usual, Ned proved he could keep his face straight longer than me, and I burst into laughter.

'You know one of the reasons I like you, Ned?'

'Wassat?'

'You talk an even bigger load of rubbish than I do.'

He laughed himself, and pulled on another sock. As usual we were happy just to talk together. It had been a good and lasting friendship. Now – well, I was going to have a jolly good go at busting it up.

'Ned . . . you know about you're being best man . . .'

'Aha!' He dived into his locker, and emerged with a thin blue book. 'I've been reading all about it.'

'Eh?'

'They bring round a library,' he explained. 'On a trolley. I ordered this.'

Of course – the cultural version of meals-on-wheels. Fiction-in-motion. Or, if the hospital librarian is sufficiently broad-minded, muck-on-a-truck. Ho, ho. But this book wasn't funny. Because it meant Ned was taking the whole thing quite seriously. Damn, damn, damn.

'Ah, good,' I told him. 'Now look . . .'

'And my brother says,' he interrupted, 'that the best man makes it with the bridesmaid.'

'Pardon?'

'Who's that going to be, Jim?' He rubbed his hands in anticipation. Perhaps I should be glad it was just his hands.

'I don't think that's actually *obligatory*, Ned. You know, more of an optional extra.'

'Boy, I can't wait!' He found an ancient Mickey Mouse t-shirt and pulled it on. 'I love weddings. See, I never thought you'd have the full works, Jim. It's just great. We're losing the knack of all that. I thought we'd all be down the registry office in kaftans and dark glasses.'

I blushed. We'd both gone through that stage. Believe me, it's only when you feel the wind whistle up your caftan that you fully appreciate the genius of the man who invented trousers.

'Those days are long gone, Ned.'

'I fear so,' he said tragically. 'We shall not see their like again. You know . . .' confidential again, 'I actually saw someone smoke a joint the other day.'

I whistled in surprise. 'Go on!'

He nodded. 'Brought tears to the eyes.' I wasn't surprised. It always brought tears to my eyes, too.

'Oh well.' Ned sighed. 'Tempus fidgets, the wheel has come full-circle. Burton shares are looking up, and we're all back in narrow-leg trousers.'

I took up the theme. 'The barber's clippers are being dusted off and the shops are full of pointed shoes. D'you know, I read in the *Standard* the other day, Mick Jagger's going bald!'

'No!'

Together, we mourned the passing of our youth, our generation.

Me first, 'The generation that gave you . . . ,' with awe, 'The Beatles!'

Ned, ditto, 'Joe Cocker!'

Me, 'The Rolling Stones!'

Then Ned, with derision, 'I mean . . . The Bee Gees!'

Me, ditto, 'Rubbish!'

Him, 'Abba.'

Me, 'Don't make me laugh!'

Him, 'The Commodores.'

Me – with considerable surprise – 'Who?'

'They're a group.'

'I've never heard of them.' Well – have you?

I looked down at my mate, as he sat half-dressed on his hospital bed. I better tell him, I thought. He looked up, and he saw it in my face. We'd been friends for a very long time, and he knew. He knew.

'Fran doesn't want me to be best man, does she?'

I owed him the truth. 'No.'

Short silence, notable for its lack of comfort.

'See,' I began, 'what we have here is an ongoing clash of loyalties situation.'

Ned didn't laugh. 'Well, what I reckon . . .'

'Yeah?'

'You owe me one more go, Captain.'

I did. Of course I did. How could there ever be any doubt? I needed a best man, and Ned was, literally, my best man. He was, as some Americans still say, 'my man'. I didn't have a choice, I didn't *want* a choice. Ned would be my best man. And I wouldn't argue about who Fran chose as bridesmaid. So there.

'Right on, mate,' I told Ned. 'Right on.'

Ned knew a big decision when he heard it. He looked shy for a moment, and burrowed in his locker again, coming up with a rather elderly-looking pair of underpants.

'I won't stay while you get dressed,' I said, retreating. 'People are talking about us quite enough as it is. See you outside.'

'Jim' – he stopped me.

'Mmm?'

'I won't make a heavy speech at the wedding.'

'Never thought you would, mate.'

'Didn't you?' He looked sideways at me.

'Yes, I did,' I confessed. 'Yes, I was lying just then. I'm getting quite good at it, you should've heard me tell that nurse about Tehran.'

That threw him. 'Eh?'

'See you.' I went back out to the reception desk. And Sister.

'Miss Nightingale . . . ?'

'My name is Patterson, Mr Shelley. Mrs Julia Patterson. Don't you think it just a trifle passé to call nurses Florence Nightingale?'

Passé? Touché. I do hate to be thought old-fashioned.

'Jim,' I introduced myself. 'How do you do. I've come to apologise.'

She smiled and waited.

'Um . . . I think you do a fantastic job for scandalous reward.' Quite true. 'I'm sorry if I was rude – I just don't want it getting out about the bike sheds. And if I'm ill I'll ask to come here so you can get your own back, and I won't need to feel guilty any more.'

There – for an apology, that was quite handsome, wasn't it?

'Are you always so masochistic?' Sister asked.

'Listen, it was a toss-up between layabout and self-flagellant.'

'So you're a layabout, are you?'

'Well, a failed layabout. I got a job.'

'Oh, I'm sorry.' Oodles of fake sympathy. 'How awful for you.'

'Yeah, well, plenty of disappointments in life.'

'You're taking it very well.'

'Thank you.' I do meet 'em, don't I!

I tried a new line on her, 'Nice dress.'

She rustled her regulation starched uniform. 'Thank you. I got it from a little lady in Bond Street.'

'She's a treasure.'

'Do you like the matching hat?'

'Knockout!'

We grinned at each other. Peace was made. Past offences forgiven and forgotten. Like I said before – wasn't she something!

Behind me I heard the pad-pad-pad of baseball boots. Ned arrived.

'Okay, Jim, I'm ready.'

'Great.'

Ned turned to Sister. 'Thank Jenny for me, love, will you?'

'Sure.'

'And I'll see you tomorrow at The Sticky Rib.'

'Eight o'clock,' she confirmed.

I opened my mouth, nearly said something stupid, shut my mouth just in time. Ned leaned forward and kissed Sister on her full rich lips. She kissed him back. Stone me! And I thought *I* was getting on well!

'Goodbye, Mr Shelley.' No kiss for me. 'Send us a card from Tehran.'

We went, Ned walking jauntily, me stumbling at his side.

'What's all this Tehran stuff?'

Bugger Tehran, what about Sister?

'She's married, Ned,' I pointed out.

'They're the best!'

I shook my head in despair. 'There's just no standards today.'

'You're only jealous.'

That's typical of Ned. Resorting to the truth again.

The Red Lion was just as noisy that evening, but it appeared, on the surface, to be more peaceful. Just as well. Fran was with me. If there was a fight, and she was watching, I'd *have* to be heroic. But peace reigned. I bought halves for us both, and we found seats at the same corner table. Why halves? Well, Ned was due to join us, and that meant a long evening. I wasn't looking forward to it, either. The best man crisis had still to be resolved. If I stuck to my decision, I was bound to hurt Fran.

If I switched, I'd hurt Ned. And myself. If we tried to talk it out there'd be a row between the three of us. I said a very rude word under my breath, and drank a very great deal of my half of Old and Awful. Delicious. At least, in this changing and difficult world, there is always beer.

Fran and I chatted to each other in a manner which I think is described as desultory. Neither of us listened to what the other was saying. Fran said something about her work. I said something about mine. We both knew what we had to talk about.

I decided to get it over with. 'Fran . . .'

She beat me to it. 'You still want Ned for best man, don't you?'

She'd known me for a very long time, too.

'Every time I'm about to say something, people tell me what it is,' I protested. 'I must have a liquid crystal print-out on my forehead.'

She waited. I had another quick bash at the brew, then I got on with it.

'The proposed terms are as follows: he won't make a heavy speech at the wedding. We have absolute power of veto, on what he says and how he plans to behave. He is to smile, with a convincing appearance of warmth, at your father on at least three separate occasions. He will reduce his alcohol intake by fifty per cent over the actual period of the ceremony. He is to eschew all words of a sexual or quasi-religious nature. In any descriptions of the functions of his body or its products he is to employ euphemisms or accepted medical terminology, viz: Will you excuse me, not: I'm dying for a slash. Or: I find myself out of sympathy with your remarks, not: Why don't you get . . .'

Fran stopped me. 'Yes, I see.'

Privately, I thought that if Ned fulfilled all those conditions neither of us would recognise him. I waited for Fran's verdict. It came.

'Fine. That's okay then.'

'Do you say that whole-heartedly?'

'No,' she admitted. 'But I'll work at it.' A smile. 'It's cool, Shelley.'

I gave her a quick kiss. Then a long slow one. I felt a lot better. And she felt delicious.

Ned broke up the snogging session. 'All right, all right, that's enough of that. You're not married yet.'

I got to my feet. 'What would you like, Squire?'

'Pint.' He turned to Fran. 'Hello, Fran, how are you?'

'Fine, Ned. You?'

Splendid! They were on speaking terms. I made for the bar, thought about something halfway across the carpet, and came back.

'Uh . . . Fran,' I said loudly and meaningfully. 'I quite fancy a Scotch egg with mine, they look really good.'

She missed it for a moment. Then she saw me looking at Ned as he pulled up a chair. The evening sun was streaming through the window, and shining right through his ribs. A draught came under the door, blew him off his feet, and into his chair. Fran caught on.

'Good idea. Have they got those nice crusty ham rolls?'

'I'll get you one,' I told her, all gluttonous enthusiasm. Then – 'Ned?'

'Eh?'

'Fancy something with your pint?'

'Oh, thanks, Jim, yeah. I'll have a whisky.'

I gave up and got the drinks. When I came back with a trayful, it was all sweetness and light around the table. Fran had clearly told Ned she okayed his appointment as best man. Now they were chatting away happily. They might almost be friends. Perhaps that's what they were – almost friends.

Ned took his pint. 'Here's to married life!'

We drank.

'And parenthood,' he went on. 'Blimey, I'd never thought of you two being dynastic.'

'We're not dynastic,' I told him, with a meaningful glance at Fran. 'We're careless.'

She kicked me on the ankle. Serve me right.

'Shall we talk about something else?' she suggested.

'Okay.' As it happened, there was something we had to talk about. Urgently, too. 'Ned – you know that guy who hit you?'

'I'm not likely to forget.' He sank his whisky.

'You know how, when the police collared him, he said if he ever saw me or you again he'd kill us?'

'Yeah.'

'Well . . . ' I pushed back my chair, 'He's just walked in.'

SIXTEEN

I WOKE early. The night before had been a little heavy on the fruit of the hop, and a quick trip to the bathroom was a priority.

Relieved, and teeth-cleaned, I padded back and sat on the side of our bed. I wasn't sleepy. The day ahead promised to be fraught with problems – so many, in fact, that despite the sight of the delectable Fran, fast asleep in an exotic pose and a rucked-up nightie, I didn't even feel randy. Instead I felt twitchy.

So I sat there and calmed myself by looking at Fran as objectively as possible. I felt I'd done a lot for the lady over the past weeks and months. For her I had battled with Mrs H., and won us a roof over our heads. For her I had taken up gainful employment. For her I had put money in a building society, made wedding plans, trifled with my best friend. I'd done it all for her. I was either in love, or loopy. I looked at her more closely. She was one of the few women in the world who look as lovely asleep as they do awake. No, I wasn't loopy.

Into the kitchen, up to the fridge, and out with the plastic packet of orange juice. I opened the thing, not without a struggle, and poured two glasses. I drank one. It was cold and acidy, and after a moment I felt much better.

The day was going to be a long one. At lunchtime we were due to entrain for Outer Britain. We were going to a part of the country which, until recently, I never even knew existed. There we were to meet and stay with Fran's father. Something else I was doing just for Fran. For a moment I felt a strong surge of justifiable pride in my own courage and self-sacrifice. Then that went, and I was left feeling twitchy again.

I picked up the other glass of orange juice, and went back into the main room. Fran had disappeared under a mound of blankets. That usually meant she was ready to wake up. I sat down beside the mound, and gently lifted a blanket. One brown eye looked back at me.

'Orange juice,' I whispered.

'Mmm?' She struggled to a sitting position, pushed the hair out of her eyes, took the glass and sipped. 'Mmm . . .'

'Breakfast?' I was still whispering.

'Mmm.'

'Eggs? Toast? Coffee?'

She nodded.

'Okay.' Still a whisper.

She put a hand on my arm, and whispered herself, 'Why are you whispering?'

'In case I wake you.'

Fran grunted with justifiable contempt for such a weak joke so early in the morning. She handed me her empty glass, turned over, and settled down for a secondary kip.

I sat at the table. There were two piles of paper in front of me. One was blank, and the other was filled with Fran's neat and yet somehow flamboyant handwriting. This was her novel, half-finished and as yet unread. No wonder she was sleepy. She'd sat up half the night working on it, instead of being sensible and coming down to the pub with me. For the umpteenth time I wondered if it was any good. I desperately hoped so. But I wouldn't know until I'd read it. Just a bit of it . . .

I tried to resist the temptation. I wrestled with the Devil for some five seconds. Then I gave in, picked up the top sheet, and began reading. I read the words 'Sarah stumbled slightly as she left the train, and her heavy case . . .' and then I was rudely interrupted.

'Put my book down!'

She'd caught me at it. She'd seen me, through three blankets and a sheet. Amazing.

I dropped the paper as if it was alight. 'Sorry, no, I was just . . .'

Fran sat up. She was livid. 'Oooo, you do annoy me about that!'

'Yes . . . you see . . .'

'I've *told* you, I can't bear people seeing it before it's finished. You'll be the first to read it when I *have* finished, until then please have the common decency to *leave it alone*!'

Phew!

'You're awake then.' I tried a bright smile.

Fran tried a filthy look.

'I just take an interest, you know,' I told her.

'Interest? You've got a nose like a Jewish elephant.'

I stood up. Frankly, I considered that last remark a discriminatory slur on three of today's persecuted minorities – the Jews, the elephants, and the Shelleys – but this was no time for a discussion on racial and animal prejudice. So I just said, rather stiffly, 'I'll cook the breakfast,' and went into the kitchen.

I opened the fridge again and looked around. Fran called from the bed, her tone a little more conciliatory.

'We could have some spinach with the eggs.'

'What?'

'Well, as we're going away – it might go off. Might as well use it up.'

I checked the fridge again. 'I hope you don't apply that principle too freely,' I replied. 'There's mayonnaise, stilton and chocolate mousse in here.'

The thought made me feel sick. I felt even sicker when I realised we were out of milk. I went back into the main room, and pulled on my usual gear – t-shirt, jeans, leather jacket.

Fran woke from a second doze. 'Where're you going?'

'No milk.'

I got safely to the door before I tried a parting shot.

'Besides,' – I tapped my nose significantly – 'I promised Sabu I'd meet him at the synagogue.'

Something heavy thumped against the door as I closed it behind me.

Back in the good old days, when times were right and people behaved properly and civilisation wasn't crumbling around our ears – about two years ago, to be precise – the shop on the corner was a general grocery, and it sold everything. But now it had become a health food shop. It sold only about a quarter of the range of the old grocery, but it made up for that deficiency by charging four times as much. Behind the counter was a thin, yellowy lady, who greeted my appearance with a warm and friendly blank stare and a rather fruity cough.

'You're open early,' I began with a bright smile.

'Been open an hour.'

All healthy people get up early. Fact of life. Didn't you know?

'Have you got any milk?'

'Goats, Channel Islands, or Vegetable?'

What, no coconut? 'Channel Islands, please.'

She disappeared for some time. I supposed she'd gone to Jersey for it. In the meantime I examined the other produce on display. A cardboard box featured one ancient cabbage, which looked like a mummy's head. An *unwrapped* mummy's head. A sort of deathly green, with holes and flaps. Next to it was a box of severed mummy's fingers. A price tag boasted that the tatty head was worth thirty-eight pence, and the fingers bore a notice that read, 'Carrots. 40p per lb.'

A cough drew near. The lady reappeared with my carton of milk.

'Is that right?' I asked her, pointing at the cabbage. 'Thirty-eight pence?'

She nodded. 'They're grown in compost.'

I pointed at the carrots. 'What are these grown in? Yeti droppings?'

She was not amused. 'Anything else?'

I thought rapidly. What were we having for breakfast? Eggs? Right then, for that we'd need . . . eggs!

'I'd like six eggs please . . . um, how much are they?'

'Forty-eight pee.'

'For *six*?'

'Yes. They're free-range.'

'Free-range what? Ospreys?'

She was even more unamused, and gave me an aggressive cough.

'Look, they're not ordinary eggs.'

'I don't care if they're a limited edition, signed by the hen,' I told her. 'I'll skip the eggs. Will you take a cheque for the milk?'

She extended a hand that trembled, with either anger or ill health. Possibly both.

'Fourteen pee please.'

'Thank you.' I gave her the cash. 'Sally Oppenheim's got no idea what it's like up here at the front.'

I left, pursued by a volley of bronchial blasts.

Fran spent the morning on her book. If I trespassed within ten feet, I was accused of reading over her shoulder. Eventually I was driven out to the pub. No, you're right – it doesn't take much.

'The Victory' had suffered a defeat. The Fo'c'sle, of which I had been temporary Captain, was The Snug again. And – thanks to pressure in the form of stickers, affixed to the keg taps and reading 'Gnat's Pee' – the management had taken a small step back towards good taste, and re-introduced some real beer. It was called 'Super Cask', it was a blatant attempt by the big brewery combines to cash in on the trend to real ale, it wasn't very good, and it was grossly over-priced. But I drank it.

Maggie, the barmaid with the bosom, was still there. She pulled me a pint, then rested her perfect pair on her folded forearms, and watched me scribbling in my notebook.

'What are you writing, Shelley?'

'A love story.' It was work, actually. More a sort of love-of-money story.

'Go on!'

'The eternal triangle. All about this windscreen called Wendy.'

'What?'

'And there are two men in her life – Willie Wiper, who's wet and scratchy, and Walter Wiper, a gay young blade who's dry and a real smoothie. Wendy just loves being wiped down by

Walter, but she *hates* Willie. He's probably got bad breath as well.'

Maggie grew concerned about my mental health. 'Are you all right?'

I explained in tedious detail about the advertising agency's new account – a car components firm – and about my brief to brighten up the image of windscreen wipers and other assorted bits of car, none of which meant anything to a pedestrian like me.

'Actually, Mags, you could help me here. Give me the woman's angle. If you were a windscreen – I mean, a really sexy bit of triple-zoned laminate, what would you look for in a wiper?'

'Dunno. Why don't you ask Fran?'

'Ah, she's too deeply into pure art right now to be bothered.'

Not that I'd ask her, anyway. Fran's reaction would be one of total contempt for both wiper-blades. Much the same as mine. Oh well . . .

Maggie wanted to know about Fran's 'pure art'.

'She's writing a book.'

'What about?'

'Life.'

'That's funny.'

'What?' Maggie usually took everything so seriously.

'I was thinking about that only the other day.'

Ah, she meant life was funny-peculiar. That figured.

'I mean, I was thinking, "What *is* it all about? The world, and the stars, and everything, and us?" '

There. Who says young people aren't intellectual?

'What are we *doing* here?' she insisted.

'I'm writing plays about wiper-blades.'

'No, I don't mean that . . . '

'I know what you mean, Maggie.' Stop being so condescending, Shelley. At least she tries.

'Well, what do you think?'

'I don't.' I decided to lighten the conversation. 'My mother warned me about thinking. If God had meant us to think, He'd have given us brains, she'd say as she stroked my golden hair with a hand as white as Arum Lilies. What a woman!'

Maggie thought about this, then asked, 'Was she very clever, Shelley?'

'Thick as a cowpat. The mental capacity of a dead traffic warden.'

I thought that was rather neat.

'You say some terrible things,' Maggie said.

'It's a gift. Never had a lesson in my life.'

'She still alive?'

I nodded. 'She's in Scotland with her boyfriend.'

Maggie clearly thought that Mothers are fat floury-elbowed old ladies in aprons. 'You're having me on.'

'No, she's a young woman,' I explained. 'She had me very early. Very early indeed. Always says that's why I turned out so foul. Her eggs weren't ready.'

'What does your father say about that?'

'Not a lot. He died three years ago.'

'Oh!'

She was shocked and I was ashamed. That was a cheap verbal trick to play on someone like Maggie. I could do better than that.

'Not that he could've said much, he ran off with our daily woman to celebrate my passing the eleven-plus. He thought such academic precocity could only lead to a knighthood and a life of lotus-eating gentility. So, his responsibility to me discharged, he left in search of a new life with Mrs Wilkins.'

Maggie giggled, a little nervously. 'I think you make half of this up.'

'Only half?'

Yes, I do invent. At least, I augment. But there's no need. There's no need ever to make anything up. Reality is already unbelievable.

'So did your mother bring you up?'

Well – she asked for it. She was going to get it. The complete story. I talked rapidly, to forestall interruptions.

'She likes to think so. In fact, in one so young, motherhood of necessity jostled for place beside the agonies of her own adolescence. Motherhood came off a bad second. Many's the night I had to sit up with her, sorting out her problems – boy-friends, spots, what to wear on dates – you know the kind of thing – holding her hand all night when Buddy Holly died, nail-varnishing the ladders in her Tangier beige fifteen denier Bear brand . . . '

I ran out of breath, and Maggie jumped in. Her fears for my mental stability had been revived.

'I think you ought to see a doctor.'

'The real trouble,' I continued, 'started when the Sixties began to swing. She espoused the cause of permissiveness with a revivalist fervour. In every way. At university I spent all my grant bailing her out on pot-smoking charges. She grows it to this day – her flat's like Kew Gardens, littered with gro-bags of Lebanese Gold wilting in the Habitat spotlights. She gives it to people in tea. The vicar came one day, and he's been back every day since. I think he thinks he had a direct contact with Head Office. Ever after his sermons give the term High Church new meaning.'

Sometimes I can make myself laugh, and this was one of those times. I grinned and Maggie relaxed. So it wasn't true about my parents, it was only a joke.

Ah, if only it was . . .

'Does your mother know you're getting married?' Maggie asked.

'Daren't tell her. The disappointment will kill her.'

I looked at my watch. Time to go. I drained my pint. Willie Wiper and his mate would have to wait. Fran's father wouldn't.

I told Maggie that when I came back, she could tell me all about *her* mother. I felt I owed her something. After all, I'd used her shamefully. Fran was too busy to be talked at. I'd promised to be nice and polite with Fran's Dad. I had to rattle off at someone, and Maggie was convenient.

And after all, isn't that what barmaids are for?

SEVENTEEN

WE BOTH worked on the train.

Correction. Fran worked, scribbling away at her opus in a loose-leafed folder. I tried to work, but I found it strangely illogical to be worrying about bits of cars while travelling by train. So instead I looked out of the window for a while. I saw dozens of cows, and none of them were worrying about how to sell wiper-blades. Lucky buggers.

After a while looking out of the window became boring, so I decided to talk to Fran instead. She herself didn't want to talk. But after all, that was only *her* opinion.

'You gonna be famous?' I began.

She gave me a look of irritation, then looked around to make sure no one had heard.

We were in one of those modern open-plan carriages, seats in groups of four with tables, and a passage down the middle. Like a toastrack. British Rail seem to have abandoned the old-style compartments, and I'm not surprised. After all, they had two major faults. They were comfy, and people liked them. Well, we can't have comfort or popularity on British Rail. So there we were, stuck in a toastrack. Fortunately, very few people want to go to the part of the country where Fran's father lives. Very few people have even *heard* of it. So the train was half empty, and we were alone.

'The Erica Jong of West Hampstead?' I suggested, and got another look from Fran in reply.

'You see,' I continued, 'I don't think I could cope with that.'

'What?' She looked up, puzzled.

'If you became an internationally-famous author, while I was still sweating over the song of the wiper-blades,' I explained.

'What?' A note of rancour crept into her voice.

I waited until she'd begun writing again, then – 'I suppose I'm slandered.'

That did it. She closed the folder, gave me the patient smile of those accustomed to dealing with the stupid, and waited for me to go on. I did.

'All my bad points, set up to be knocked down by some invincibly witty female, eh?' I guessed.

'What are you talking about?'

'In the book.'

'You're not in it!'

'What?'

With acknowledgement to Oscar Wilde, I would like to say that there is only one thing worse than being in a novel your girlfriend has written, and that's not being in a novel your girlfriend has written. I couldn't believe it. How could she leave me out? It was like . . . forgetting my birthday. No, worse – it was like forgetting my name!

'You're not in it,' she said again. 'Why should you be?'

Well . . . she had a point.

'You know . . . ' I flannelled. 'Major influence in your life . . . ' I felt silly.

'Who? You?' said Fran with considerable scorn. I felt sillier.

'Yes, me. Remember?' I had to protest. 'Me, the one who's related to the child you're going to have. Your father's son-in-law to be. The breakfast cooker.'

What a reference!

'You could be in it, actually,' Fran said, surprised at herself. 'I hadn't really thought. I could model the art teacher on you.'

'Yeah?' I liked the idea of that. Arty, a bit hippy, pulling all the birds.

'No . . . ' She changed her mind. 'No, he's . . . '

'What?'

'Well, not really you.'

'I suppose,' I said with cold irony, 'he's too charming, intelligent and stunning a lover to be me.'

'Exactly.' She grinned. 'I'll try you for the caretaker at the end.'

'That would no doubt be the consummately boring mental defective with BO you mentioned?'

'Yeah.'

Game, set, and match to Fran. I gave up and looked out of the window. More cows. They didn't have girlfriends who were wittier than them. Lucky buggers.

We were interrupted by a genuine British Rail steward. He wore a grubby white coat, he needed a shave, and he carried a tray on which was stacked dozens of paper cups, plus some genuine British Rail sandwiches.

'Tea or coffee?' he asked.

So they actually brought the stuff round these days! Couldn't persuade people to queue up for it any more, I guessed.

'Coffee, please,' Fran told me.

'One of each, please,' I told the steward.

He put two cups on our table. I looked in mine. There was something at the bottom, something powdery and unpleasant.

'There's some dirt in this cup,' I pointed out.

'That's the tea.'

'What?'

'The steward'll be along in a minute, with the hot water, sir.'

Have you noticed how the word 'sir' is no longer a courtesy title? And that nowadays it's a gratuitous insult?

I looked in Fran's cup. More muck in that.

'That's coffee?'

'Yes, sir.'

'How do you know?'

'It's written on the cups.'

'So it is.' And it was. It gave me an idea. I reached up, and tapped a finger against one of his packets of sandwiches.

'See this pack of yellow polystyrene sandwiches?'

'What?'

'Could you write "Coq au vin with asparagus tips" on it? I fancy a good meal.'

The steward worked up a twisted grimace. 'You're a comedian, aren't you, sir!'

'Written on my shirt, is it?'

We looked at each other. I decided to leave it there. After all, he was just a steward, he didn't make the rules. He was probably a nice chap. And what's more, he was bigger than me.

'How much?'

'Thirty pence, please.'

I gave him fifty. 'Keep the change.'

'Thank you, sir.' He went.

Fran gave me a head-on-one-side look. 'What's the matter, Shelley?'

'I'm nervous,' I admitted.

'I know. Why?'

'Approaching the Hall of the Mountain King.'

'You're not frightened, surely?'

Was I? I wasn't sure. 'Well, I have a natural dislike of being loathed quite so virulently,' I began. 'That is to say, if you detest someone, and they reciprocate warmly, you don't normally plan to spend weekends together. Especially deep in enemy heartland. Your father and I have an admirably stable relationship, based on mutual interest. Given the chance, we'd each have the other tortured to death.'

I got quite worked up saying this, and the second steward made me jump.

'Excuse me, sir!'

I leaned back, and the steward – a shorter, spotty one – poured hot water into our cups. It turned grey.

'Is that real water?' I questioned.

He smiled without looking at me. ''Fraid so, sir. But the backroom boys are working on it. Thank you.'

He moved on. Fran sniggered. I ignored her. If the guy was that quick, what was he doing working as a train steward? I returned to the subject of our stay with Fran's dad.

'Oh well . . . I'll just spend all the time locked in our room, I suppose,' I told her.

'What do you mean, our room?'

'Eh?' What did she mean, what did I mean, our room?

'We won't be together.'

'What?'

'We'll be separated.'

She couldn't mean it. 'Separated? Don't be silly.'

'We will.' She did mean it.

'But he must know we sleep together.'

'Well, it's one of those things you don't acknowledge.'

Jesus! I could feel my eyebrows climbing ever-higher up my forehead.

'But you're having a baby,' I reminded her. 'What does he think we did? Get the vet in?'

She shrugged. 'I just know we'll be separated. It's always like that.'

'What do you mean, it's always like that? I've never been to your place before . . . Oh! I see.' I'd walked right into this one. 'Rodney.'

She nodded.

Rodney is a character who need not concern us for long. He was Fran's one previous important lover. Her taste has improved since then. He was tall and thin and he worked in Lincolns Inn, training to be a crook. He played a lot of squash, nothing wrong with that perhaps, but personally I think the bit he enjoyed was the showers with the chaps afterwards. There was something very odd about him. He drank Campari, even when he had to pay for it himself. He drank beer when he was thirsty – a criminal waste of good beer, that. He read books on Egyptology – I know because he left some with Fran – and he made notes in the margins arguing with the author. I'm not jealous of him. But I was glad to hear that when he'd visited Father he'd been 'separated'. I'd separate him. From his head, if necessary.

I looked across at Fran. She was reading something she'd written, and smiling at it. A thought struck me. I bet Rodney was in her bloody book.

I stopped looking at Fran, and looked out of the window again. A plentitude of cows, none of whom had previous lovers to worry about. Lucky buggers.

I had to admit, the house was beautiful. Brick walls, red tiles, creepers, and lots of small staircases, surprising rooms, twists and turns. Parts of it were ancient and other parts were very modern, but the two blended as smoothly as Guinness and champagne, proving once again that, despite so much evidence to the contrary, an architect is not necessarily an idiot. We came down the gravel drive, in our taxi from the station, and walked around the house to a big French window. This let us in to a passage, which in turn led into the most magnificent kitchen I have ever found in a private house. It had cupboards of pine – real pine all the way through, that is – plus a gleaming double sink, a long scrubbed table, an absolutely splendid Aga, and row upon row of copper pans. Very traditional – and yet it was also the kitchen of someone who loves all foods. I noticed a wok, and the spice racks would have made all Asia's teeming millions feel at home.

I'm the cook in the family, of course. So while I poked about amid jars of beans and pickled beetroot, Fran told me she'd go and find somebody, and she wanted the loo as well. I was alone for about five seconds before the back door opened, and a strange woman walked in.

'Ah,' she said. 'You must be . . .'

I waited. Who must I be? She still hesitated, until I had to supply the information myself.

'Shelley. James Shelley.'

'Alice Godard,' she introduced herself. 'How d'you . . .'

'How d'you do.'

She was a nice-enough looking lady – a little fat, a little past her best, with nice short brown hair and a bright smile. But she somehow gave the impression of being vague, bemused, not quite in step with life.

'Now I have got it right, haven't I?' she asked. 'You are the one who's going to marry . . .'

Long pause. I supplied the answer. 'Fran. Frances. Smith.'

'Yes. Do . . . err . . .' She waved at a chair.

'Thank you.' I sat down, feeling rather unnerved.

'Did you have a nice . . . ?'

A nice what? Day? Breakfast? Cuddle last night?

'Journey?' I guessed. Yes, that was it. 'Fine.'

'Good. Lovely day.'

'Yes. Yes, it is.'

'Mind you, it might . . . it might . . .'

'Rain?' I tried.

'Later,' she agreed.

It was weird. I felt as if I was a contestant in some appalling television game show, called perhaps 'Guess The Word!' My task was to supply the end of each sentence. If I got it right, the game proceeded. If I got it wrong, a hooter would hoot, a burper would burp, Terry Wogan would rock with simulated mirth, and I'd lose ten quid.

'But it might not,' said Alice. Rain, she meant.

'No,' I agreed.

She looked out through the big window over the sink. Fields stretched away down to a river. Woods rose on the far side. It was very quiet.

'It *is* beautiful here, isn't it?' she said with assurance.

'Stunning.' It was.

'Nowhere like . . .'

Here we went again. 'England?'

'Nowhere in the whole . . .'

'World?' Yes. I was scoring well.

'Yes, especially in the . . .'

'Summer!' I was winning!

'Would you like a . . .'

'Cup of tea?'

Wrong! Hoot! Burp! Studio laughter. Take away a tenner.

The correct answer, it appeared, was 'Wash or something?'

'Ah, well,' I began in reply, 'I rather think . . . err . . .'

'Frances,' she supplied.

'Might be in the . . .' I continued.

'Bathroom,' she finished.

'Aha.' Something had gone wrong. She was no longer doing it to me. I was doing it to her.

Further disjointed conversation followed. We learned that Mr Smith was not in, a fact for which she was very sorry, and I wasn't. Apparently he was working with an estate agency. Bully for him.

'You're doing something *now*, aren't you?' she eventually asked.

I ignored the overtones in the word 'now', and told her, 'I'm conducting a sociological survey of wiper-blades.'

'How fascinating.'

Both my remark and her response were classic conversation-stoppers. So we stopped, and looked rather helplessly at each other. Fortunately, Fran reappeared before either of us could have a nervous collapse.

'Hello, Mrs Godard.'

Oh-oh. I knew that tone. Fran's frosty freezer. Catch a blast of that, and you can warm your hands on an icicle.

'Do call me Alice, Frances.'

Phew! Alice was fighting fire with fire. Or rather, ice with ice.

'Alice,' said Fran obediently. It sounded as if the word was something nasty on the end of her tongue.

And then they kissed, with the warmth that only genuine hypocrisy can generate.

'Daddy . . . ?' Fran queried.

'Not back yet.'

'Ah.'

'Well . . .' Alice made vague motions to leave. 'If you . . .'

'Of course!' we both assured her.

'I'll just . . .' More gestures at the door.

'Please. Of course.' We chorused.

She was almost through the door when she began: 'I gather *you're* going to . . .'

'Cook?' Fran continued. 'Well, I usually do. When I'm . . .'

'Home!' I completed.

It must be catching.

This last exchange had a special significance, which didn't strike home with me until later that afternoon. Fran cook? Fran – the girl who can't boil water without getting lumps in it? Cook for us all?

We were back in the kitchen, and alone. And apart from the culinary question, there was something else I wanted to know.

'So what's Mrs Godard then?'

'Housekeeper.'

'Ah.' Was she indeed!

Fran read my mind. 'I mean, I don't know, maybe they do. It's not the sort of thing you can talk about.'

'No.' True enough.

'Daddy's certainly taken quite a shine to her.'

Taken a shine? Hmmm . . . I tried it out, 'Webster's Glint – the polish that takes a shine to your car!'

I looked at Fran. She shook her head. Oh well . . .

'So what are you going to cook?' I asked rather cruelly.

'You cook, Shelley. You do it so much better than me.'

'Motorway cafés do it better than you!' I do so enjoy doing something better than Fran, as I'm afraid I rub it in. 'I wish you'd just try sometimes.'

'I will,' she promised, a little pathetically.

I gave in. 'What'll we have?'

'Well, there's always eggs, chicken or a rabbit, but . . .'

'Great! I'll do that poached chicken you like. Where is it?'

As I said those last few words, a faint suspicion began to dawn. It strengthened when Fran pointed at the back door, with something like a snigger. And it was confirmed when, now that I listened carefully, I could hear a faint 'cluck cluck' from the garden.

'You're kidding!'

'Nope.'

I had further thoughts. 'I suppose the rabbit is that shotgun hanging on the wall.'

It was.

I sighed. 'The really bad thing about this moment,' I told Fran, 'is that I know you're not lying. I remember when Clive and Miriam got into self-sufficiency, and you put them down by telling them how your father has been into it since rationing.'

I was struck by another thought. 'This is a test, isn't it? My manhood in question?'

'Don't be silly, Shelley.'

'I suppose Rodney stuck a few pigs while he was here,' I suggested bitterly.

'You're joking. He wouldn't kill a fly unless there was a Catholic priest present.'

That made me feel a little better. Not a lot. A little.

'I'm not assassinating a chicken,' I vowed. 'Nor yet gunning down an unarmed rabbit.'

'You eat meat, Shelley,' she pointed out, but I'd been through this argument many times.

'I pay the butcher conscience money.'

'You're always saying we should face our responsibilities.'

'I'm a hypocrite. I've always been honest about that.'

But Fran had one more shot in her locker. 'Well, don't worry, Daddy'll do it. You're not expected to. I'll ask him. Or would you like to?'

Terrific! Would Daddy come and do the man's work, because his weedy snivelling son-in-law isn't up to it! I should co-co. I hadn't even met the man yet. Fortunately, as I always do when I really need it, I had a bright idea . . .

EIGHTEEN

FRAN'S FATHER thought the food was fabulous. He ate like there was no tomorrow – or at least, like there was no dinner tomorrow. He forked up great heaps of it, he chased oddments around the edge of his plate, he crunched massive mouthfuls, he scraped it into little piles with his knife, he spooned it, chewed it, swallowed it, and then he produced two silent but massive burps in appreciation of it.

'That was wonderful, Frances.' He picked up the wine bottle and refilled the glasses, even, by some error, putting a little in mine. 'Your cooking's improved out of all . . .'

'Recognition,' Alice supplied. She and he constantly finished each other's sentences. It made for a conversation I can only describe as symbiotic. Housekeeper? Ha-ha, I'm laughing.

Fran, the shameless and hypocritical hussy, basked in the praise. 'Thank you, Daddy,' she chirruped.

She smiled at him, and he gave her a food-flecked and gap-toothed grin in return. He was a gap-toothed sort of chap, really. Bits of him were . . . well, missing. He limped slightly. One turn-up was turned down. His trousers sagged. One fingernail was purple. He wore bi-focals, and a ginger moustache, and the length of ginger fur on his upper lip exactly matched the length of ginger fur on his sports jacket. He wasn't ugly, you understand, but on the other hand, he wasn't one of nature's Flash Harry's, either. Strangely enough, when I first met him – we'd all sat down at the kitchen table to eat, and he'd come banging in through the back door, said hello to all except me, and sat straight down – it came to me at that moment that if he'd been my age, and been brought up in my generation, he might have turned out looking something like me. After all, for us being a weirdo came easy. For his generation, it was more difficult, when one remembers that suede boots were once considered to reveal the depths of moral degeneration. I checked under the table. Yes, Fran's father wore suede boots.

But my thoughts of possibly finding some common ground between us faded as the meal progressed. Fran's father – Gordon was his name, at least that's what Alice called him – didn't spare me another glance, and pointedly ignored Fran's attempts to draw me into the general conversation. I had a feeling he would deal with me in his own time. Fair enough – if he wanted a verbal punch-up, then, as you will no doubt agree, having lasted this far with me, he'd come to the right man.

But now the meal was over. Gordon chased one last carrot around the serving dish, speared it, and ate it.

'What was it, exactly?' He asked Fran.

How would she know? She hadn't even watched me cook it. No wonder she looked stunned by the question.

Quickly I said: 'Vegetarian casserole.' My bright idea.

'Really was quite . . . ' said Alice.

'Delicious,' said Gordon. 'Carrots were . . .'

'Beautiful.'

'I killed them myself,' I put in. Gordon ignored me.

'How do you do those?' He asked Fran.

Woops! Fran's jaw dropped.

'I've been meaning to ask you that?' I teased her.

'Well . . . ' She gave me a look that was half-threat, half-appeal, and I came gallantly to the rescue.

'There was nutmeg, wasn't there?'

'Er . . . yes?'

'And . . . don't tell me . . . rosemary!'

'Yes . . . ' She was begging for more.

'Sugar and butter, of course.'

'You guessed!'

'Covered with water and boiled . . .'

'To a thick sauce!' Fran finished the recipe with a rush of relief, and gave me a grateful smile. 'Well done, Shelley.'

Alice gave her a prim smile. 'Well, you'll soon have him well . . .'

'Trained,' I completed.

'Well.' Alice gave me a generous smile that included the whole table. 'You've come along at last then.'

'Pardon?'

'Mr Right!' she announced, the way adults say 'Father Christmas!' to kids.

Oh God! I looked at Gordon. His face had fallen into the dregs of his casseroled carrots.

'We were beginning to wonder, Frances . . .' Alice blundered on.

'What?' from Fran.

'Well, you know, I think Gordon was getting a little . . .'

Looking at Alice, I reckoned Gordon was getting a little, too. But I left Fran to answer.

'Mmmm?'

'Well,' Alice explained, 'about being a Grandaddy.'

'Ah.' Clearly no one had told her.

Gordon looked up from under gingerish eyebrows that met in the middle.

'Well,' he grunted, 'that's one worry taken care of, anyway.'

A shock-horror silence prevailed. I thought I was going to laugh. The silence stretched on a little. Alice must have realised that she was up to her knees in it, because she stood up hastily.

'Well,' she said, much too brightly, 'if you're all finished, I'm off to my . . .'

'Me too!' Fran exclaimed, clambering up and over-acting a yawn.

I realised what was happening. I'm not that thick. I was being left alone with Gordon.

Oh no I wasn't . . .

'Yeah, well, I think I'll . . .'

'Stay and have a drink!'

It was an order. Yes, an order. But I didn't have to obey it. I wasn't in the army. I was a free man. I didn't have to do what some silly old fart in a furry jacket told me to do. I was going to do exactly what I wanted to do, and nothing else. So there!

'Ah, I think I'll just . . . ' I said again, half-rising.

'Stay and have a drink!!!'

I decided that what I wanted to do was to stay and have a drink.

The women said their goodnights, kissed Gordon on the cheek, and went. We were left alone.

The next silence lasted for about four years. In the end I had to say something.

'Well . . . ' I managed.

'What?'

'Well . . . ' I decided to play it straight. 'I hope you're not *too* disappointed in your daughter's choice.'

'I am.'

'Yes, I know.' I decided to play it funny. 'But I'd hoped you might be prepared to lie about it.'

Gordon sat back in his chair, emphatically and perhaps just a little alcoholically.

'I'm not disposed to spare the feelings of an unemployed layabout only out for what he can get!'

'I didn't know you'd been headmaster of a charm school.'

He reached a long arm behind him, and found a bottle on a shelf.

'Scotch?'

'Thank you.' Why not? 'Only the merest hint of cyanide in mine, please. Actually, I *do* have a job. As a matter of fact.'

He wasn't listening. Instead he concentrated on pouring a quadruple Scotch in my glass, and an even bigger one in his. Then he settled himself to tell me the facts of his life.

'Frances is my only child,' he began. 'And it will no doubt have not escaped your notice that when I die she will come into a reasonably large amount of money and property.'

'So I gather.' I was bored by this already. 'You couldn't give us any idea when that might be, could you? It would be so much easier for us to plan ahead.'

He breathed rather heavily. 'I wonder if I could prevail on you to shut it? Just for a few moments?'

'Please. My pleasure.'

'What I am about to confide may come as rather a shock to you.'

I opened my eyes wide to him, happy surprise on my face. 'You're not my natural father!?! I often wondered. My word. Mother speaks very well of you. Sends her love. She's well.'

'Shut up, man!'

I thought I better shut up. He really seemed to want to tell me something. All right, Gordon, the floor was yours.

'I have at least one thing to thank you for. What I'm about to tell you is bad news for me, but the fact that by extension it's also bad news for you sweetens it considerably. You see, I'm broke. Mortgaged to the hilt. Without an asset left. In the language of our American cousins, flat busted.'

He paused, lifted his glass, drained it. Very dramatic.

I had a belt at mine, then pulled out my wallet.

'I can let you have a fiver, and no hurry about paying it back,' I offered.

He sighed. 'Don't you ever take anything seriously?'

'Sometimes, I'm afraid. I mean, I try not to but . . . ' It occurred to me that Gordon looked a bit stricken. He might have been telling the truth. I asked him: 'You're not really hard up, are you?'

'Aha!' He wagged a triumphant finger. 'The first glimmerings of sincere feeling!'

It was something to do with the mean pleasure in his voice. Something to do with the long tiring day, something to do with the Scotch. Whatever it was, it made me lose my temper.

'Mr Smith!' He looked up, startled. I'm not surprised, I'd startled myself. 'I am not marrying your daughter for money! I know she's not up to much, but she's probably the best I'll do, and you get used to the smell after a bit.'

He was confused, and blustered: 'I'll thank you not to insult my daughter in my house.'

I got up. 'I've not insulted your daughter. Very much on the contrary. She happens to be the woman I want to marry, and that's because of the person she is, and not the opulence of her inheritance.'

Yes, I know. Traditional sloppy stuff. But I meant it, so it didn't sound quite as saccharine as it reads. Gordon's mouth was open, but he had nothing to say. It was my chance to get out.

'Now,' I told him, 'perhaps you'll show me to my dungeon. I shall be asleep the second my head hits the flagstone.'

'You know where Frances's room is.'

Blimey! He didn't mean . . .

'Ah . . . I rather thought we'd be tactfully separated.'

He poured himself another Scotch. 'A more absurd case of locking the stable door after the horse has bolted, it would be difficult to imagine.'

Well, this was a turn-up. Stupidly, I found myself thinking of nasty old Rodney.

I sat down again. 'Well,' I told Gordon, 'at least in one particular I seem to have misjudged you.'

'That's the least surprising thing you've said all evening.'

Fair enough.

'Look, the way I see it, Churchill and Hitler probably had a sneaking regard for each other,' I went on. 'Now it's true that I detest you nearly as much as you detest me, and nothing is going to send us moist-eyed and arm-in-arm down to the local to chat about old times together, but as we're stuck with each other, what about making the best of it? I mean, if Begin and Sadat made it . . . '

I ran out of steam there, and just sat and looked at him.

He proferred the bottle. 'Have another Scotch.'

'Thank you.'

'Did you cook supper?'

He'd caught me again, the cunning old . . .

'Yes.'

'Thought so. You're very good.'

I actually blushed. 'It's nice to work here. Superb kitchen. And all the stuff at its peak straight from the garden. Do you do all that?'

'Yes.'

'Alone?'

'Local chap helps. We sell a bit of produce, you see. Sign at the roadside stuff.' He was pleased at the chance to talk about it.

'That economic?' I asked. Somewhere a bell was ringing in my mind.

'Mmm?'

'I mean, you know, labour, all the insecticides, fertilizers and so on.'

He was appalled. 'Never use any of that stuff! Compost! Manure! Hard work!'

I identified the bell. Of course – the health food shop. The mummy's tatty head. The grisly orange fingers.

'Are you telling me that all that stuff is compost grown?' I checked.

'Yes.'

'How many free-range hens have you got?'

'Forty.'

Forty. Say – three dozen eggs on a good day. The shop charged forty-eight pence per half-dozen. That made . . . six eights are forty-eight . . . six fours are . . . blimey!

I took a deep breath. I had, it seemed, achieved some sort of understanding with Gordon. We had reached, shall we say, common ground. Common ground covered thickly with compost.

'D'you know,' I began, 'I think I may be able to help you . . .'

Fran was in bed. On my side of the bed, on my pillow, lay her old teddy. There was no room for me. I wasn't expected. Teddy had taken my place.

Well, to hell with that! I sat down and took off my shoes.

'You're kidding!' Fran was astounded.

'Nope.' I gave her a look that betrayed my every intention.

'Oh no – we can't here!'

'What are you talking about?' I felt low and tired. 'We've lived together for two years.'

'But that was away. Not home. Not in Teddy's bed. That's dirty.'

I felt more tired. 'Don't you turn against me, for God's sake. I feel like Willie Wiper as it is.'

'What?'

'Wet, frayed, and useless.'

I got a smile for that. 'How'd you get on with Daddy?'

'Went the distance.' I took off jeans and socks, and started fiddling with my shirt buttons. Life suddenly felt a burden. Unusual for me. Perhaps that's why I said what I did.

'You thought any more about an abortion?'

'We've been into that.' Tight-lipped.

'It's just that . . .'

'Shelley!' A warning.

'I know, I know. It's just a big thing, you know. It's not just a baby. If we water it regularly it might grow into a human being. And you know what they can be like. Quite apart from that, when it *is* a baby we won't be getting much sleep. And we'll probably have to convey most of its waste products manually to the loo. I mean, I gather poop-production is their thing. When they're not being sick and leaking everywhere.' I pointed an accusing finger. 'And you won't love me so much 'cos you'll only be interested in the kid!'

'I don't love you very much now,' Fran said, with a rather battered grin. I was not to be mollified.

'On a scale of a million and ten, that joke rates a half.'

She put a hand on my arm. 'What's wrong, Shelley?'

I sighed. Trouble was, I didn't know.

'The home crowd are getting to me, Fran. Your father would rather have slaughtered me than one of his chickens. The way that woman talks is absolutely . . .'

'Unnerving.' Fran supplied.

'And now I find my place in your bed usurped by a teddy bear. I mean, no disrespect, he's the best looking bear I've ever seen, and I bet his conversation makes Robert Robinson sound like Artoo Deetoo, I just wish he hadn't been sleeping in my bed.'

I sounded plaintive and silly to my own ears. If Fran had any sense, she'd have thrown me out. Thank heavens she's barmy.

'Take him out,' she told me.

I took Teddy by the arm, and lifted him out. His ancient voice-box croaked a protest. Poor rejected bear.

'He's no good to you anyway,' I said. 'He's missing a vital piece of biological equipment. Like all teddies.'

Fran grinned, and wanted to know more about my chat with her father.

'Well . . . ' She had to know sometime. 'He's broke, and he doesn't want you to know about it.'

'I know. I can see right through him.'

I liked that phrase. I tried it out, 'My driver can see right through me ever since I met Walter!'

Fran grinned but shook her head.

'No?' I'd never sell those bloody wipers. 'God, it's difficult, this job. Too much like working. He can see through you as well. He knew I'd cooked supper.'

'So are you chums now?'

'Détente I guess. Aren't you worried about him?'

'He'll cope,' she said confidently, and waved an arm to encompass the cottage and garden. 'It's a special kind of person who can call living like this "broke".'

I slipped my shirt off, stood up, and turned back my side of the bed. I turned it back a little too far. There was my Fran, waiting for me, Long, lovely, and perhaps just a little less slim around the middle than before. All mine. *All* mine.

'Well, there's one good thing about coming here,' I told her.

'What?'

'At least I've done better than Rodney.'